Michelle Kwan presents

Skating Dreams

The Turning Point

By Nola Thacker

Hyperion Paperbacks for Children
New York

Printed in the United States of America
First edition
1 3 5 7 9 10 8 6 4 2
This book is set in 12.5 point Life.
ISBN: 0-7868-1379-2
Visit www.hyperionchildrensbooks.com

1

"**D**id you see that? Unbelievable!" the announcer shouted. "Lauren Wing just turned in the most magnificent free-skating performance I've ever seen!"

"The crowd is going wild!" said the second announcer, her voice rising with excitement. "This has got to be the finest long program in the history of the World Championship. Let's see if the judges agree."

At center ice, I raised both hands to wave at the cheering spectators. My eyes blurred with tears. I'd worked so hard. And I had just delivered a perfect performance.

I blinked furiously. Then, still smiling, I

skated off the ice through a rain of flowers and stuffed animals from the fans. Some began to shout my name: *"Lauren! Lauren! Lauren!"*

My coach handed me the skate guards for my blades and a warm-up jacket, then escorted me to the Kiss and Cry to wait for the decision of the judges.

I heard the shout of the crowd before I focused on the numbers. I felt my coach's grip tighten around my shoulders.

"I don't believe this," I whispered.

But it was true.

"Lauren Wing has just won the gold medal," the announcer said.

"No, she hasn't! She can't!" A tall, slender girl with dark hair and angry blue eyes appeared. She pointed an accusing finger at me. "She blew her triple Lutz! That was a *two-footed* landing!" Erica Claiborn's eyes flashed. "Admit it! You *know* your other foot touched the ice."

I tried to speak. But no words came.

"You can't do a triple Lutz! I demand a replay!" cried Erica.

Someone began to boo. The cheers of the crowd turned into an angry roar.

Then an alarm went off.

"No!" gasped Lauren and woke up.

Green eyes stared into hers. Curled next to her on the pillow, Lutz, her cat, shifted his purr into a thunderous roar. The clock radio alarm buzzed nasally. Lauren rolled toward it, hand outstretched to slam it into silence, but discovered that she had wound herself up like a mummy in her sheets.

"Lauren, turn off the alarm! We're awake," her sister Lacey said from across the room. Lacey sat up, her dark, short hair sticking out in spikes all over her head. She was eight, almost two years younger than Lauren. She and Lauren and five-year-old Lisa, the youngest of the three sisters, all shared one bedroom of their three-bedroom house. Lacey and Lisa slept in bunk beds on one side of the room and Lauren slept in the bottom of a second set of bunk beds on the other side.

"Lauren!" said Lacey again. "The alarm!"

"I'm trying!" said Lauren, struggling to get an arm free. Lutz stood up and showed all his teeth in a scornful yawn. Tail high, he jumped off the bed and stalked to the door.

"Mrrow!" he said, ordering someone to open the door and let him out.

Lauren freed her arm at last and slapped it down on the clock. The alarm stopped.

"Everybody up?" called their mother, knocking on the bedroom door. She opened it and peered in.

"Mrrow-row!" growled Lutz and stalked out. Mrs. Wing stepped back and raised her eyebrows. "Good morning to you, too, Lutz," she said.

Lacey had already slid down from the top bunk. "We're up," she said.

"Good," said Mrs. Wing. She disappeared from the doorway.

"Mmm," said Lauren, trying to shake off the bad dream. And it had started out so well, too.

As Lauren yawned and stretched, Lacey reached down and patted her younger sister. "Lisa? Wake up, sleepyhead," Lacey said. Lisa stuck her head under the pillow.

Lauren wished she could do the same. But she couldn't. It was time to get ready for school. She swung her feet over the side of the bed, and stretched again.

Lisa sat up slowly. Her mouth dropped open in a jaw-cracking yawn. Her eyes were still squeezed shut.

"Stop yawning!" Lacey ordered. "Yawning is contagious. You'll make me catch it."

Lisa giggled, opened her eyes, and yawned once more. Lauren couldn't help it. She yawned, too.

"No yawn-a-thons! That's it! I'm out of here," said Lacey, and she raced out of the room toward the bathroom.

Lisa threw herself out of bed and ran over to her oldest sister. "I made you catch my yawns!" she said and giggled again.

"Silly sleepyhead gigglehead," said Lauren and hugged Lisa back. "Come on." Lauren stood up and took Lisa's hand.

As she helped Lisa get ready for school and got ready herself, Lauren kept thinking about the dream. Had it meant something? Was it a bad-luck sign?

No, she told herself firmly. It was only a dumb dream. She made a face. It was just her luck that she couldn't get away from that snooty Erica Claiborn, even in dreams—or nightmares.

"Breakfast is ready," Mrs. Wing called.

"Wait for me at the bottom," Lauren told Lisa. "Make sure I don't fall."

Lisa nodded and walked to the bottom of the stairs. She turned and looked up at Lauren.

"Ready?" asked Lauren.

Lisa nodded solemnly.

Turning around and grabbing the railing with one hand, Lauren hopped backward down the stairs with both feet, one step at a time. She had a theory that hopping up and down the stairs made her legs stronger, and in figure skating, strong legs were important.

When she got to the bottom, she turned to face Lisa. "How'd I do?" she asked.

"Six!" said Lisa, giving her sister the highest score a judge could give a skater, just as she did every morning.

"All right!" said Lauren. She scooped Lisa up and spun her around. "Now we're Torvill and Dean about to win the gold medal for ice dancing with our amazing Lisa spin!"

"Lauren," said her mother from the door of the kitchen. "Do you think you can stop skating long enough to join us for breakfast?" But she was smiling.

"Sorry, Mom," said Lauren, returning her mother's smile sheepishly.

Bryan was finishing his second bowl of oatmeal as Lisa and Lauren sat down. He drained his glass of orange juice and jumped up. "Gotta be out of here in five," he announced. "I'm meeting some guys to bag some study time before school. Test. Math."

Mrs. Wing nodded. "And a hockey game this afternoon. Your father and I are going to pick Lisa up from kindergarten, and we'll be there."

"Me, too," said Lacey.

"I'll be a little late, but I'll be there." Lauren had a skating lesson that afternoon at the Pine Creek Skating Rink, and she would go from there to the school rink to cheer on her brother and his team, the Pine Creek Otters. She grinned at her brother. "I wouldn't want to miss the Total Ice Rocket in action."

"That's *Mr.* Rocket, to fans who aren't respectful," Bryan said.

Lauren stuck out her tongue at her brother and he returned the favor. Lisa immediately stuck out her tongue, too.

"You better be careful, Lisa. Your face'll freeze like that," Lacey said.

"Will not!" Lisa said.

"Sure it will," Lacey said. "How do you think Mr. Rocket got the way he is?"

Lisa giggled, and Lacey smiled affectionately at her.

Ignoring the usual morning exchange of insults, Mrs. Wing said to Lauren, "We'll put your bike on the bike rack after the game and give you a ride home."

Lauren nodded. Normally, after her lesson, she stayed at the rink and practiced with her best skating buddies, Annie McGrath and Danielle Kurowicki. She hated missing even a single practice, especially now. Lauren was preparing for the upcoming North Atlantic Regionals. If she did well in those, she hoped her coach would agree she was ready to move up to the junior level of skating competition. From there she could move to the senior level and be eligible to try out for a place on the Olympic team.

But she'd be there to cheer Bryan on, just as he came to figure skating competitions to cheer her on, and just as they all went to Lacey's soccer games, too. Lauren looked at Lisa, who was picking her cereal out of her spoon one piece at a time with the utmost concentration. She wondered what sport Lisa would be doing when she got a little older.

"I'm gone," Bryan announced, and he was, at almost hyper-speed. That was the way Bryan did everything, and one of the reasons Lauren had christened him the Total Ice Rocket.

"And I need to get to the restaurant to start on the bookkeeping," said Mrs. Wing. "Come on, Lisa."

They finished breakfast in a familiar rush. Mrs. Wing took Lisa to kindergarten before she went to the family restaurant, where she did the accounting and Mr. Wing was the manager. He had left much earlier in the morning as he often did, to receive deliveries of food and supplies. Lacey and Lauren rode their bikes to the Pine Creek School. Lauren carried her skating gear in a duffel bag strapped to her bike rack. It weighed a lot, but she figured it helped build her stamina just as much as going up and down the stairs did. Besides, keeping a locker at the skating rink cost extra money, and the Wing family had to watch every penny. Figure skating was expensive.

At school, she stowed the bag in her school locker and tried to put figure skating out of her mind. She had to keep her grades up if she wanted to keep skating.

And more than anything else, Lauren Wing wanted to keep skating.

Forever.

2

"It's been forever! I mean, how long do you need? Puh-lease! How hard is it to do a double toe loop?" Erica put her hands on her hips and smirked at Annie McGrath.

Annie's cheeks, already red from exertion and the permanent chill that hovered above the ice of the Pine Creek Ice Skating Rink, grew even redder.

Lauren caught Danielle Kurowicki's eye and then said loudly, "It was a good try." Sometimes, Lauren thought, it seemed as if Erica never said anything nice if she could think of something nasty to say instead.

Danielle added, "Try again, Annie."

"More height this time," said their coach,

Jenna Knudson. "Use your arms for balance *and* for lift."

Annie nodded. She had a quick temper, but she was clearly determined not to lose it. She got up and skated across the ice. She stepped back onto the right outside edge of her skate, then tapped with her left toe as she propelled herself upward off her right foot. Drawing her arms toward her chest, she crossed her ankles together and spun around in the air.

Lauren held her breath as Annie landed on her right foot. Her left foot came down perilously close to the surface of the ice, but her toe didn't scrape it. She held on to her jump.

Coach Knudson nodded. "Better," she said.

"It's about time," Erica muttered.

The coach gave Erica a sharp look. Erica smiled innocently back. When Erica smiled, she looked like the nicest, kindest, sweetest person anyone would ever hope to meet.

Ha, thought Lauren. When they were handing out nice, Erica must have been in the locker room.

Annie skated back toward her friends, her lips pressed together.

"You did it," said Danielle.

"But I could have done it better," said Annie.

"That's true," agreed Erica.

Annie's brown eyes flashed, but before she could say anything, Coach Knudson said, "Your lesson is not for some time yet, Erica. I suggest you do some stretches to get warmed up."

The coach's voice was firm. Erica smiled her fake sweet smile again and said, "I don't like to practice with all these people on the ice. But you're right; I should warm up." She clomped on her skate guards away from the edge of the rink, where she had been watching the lesson.

Lauren, Danielle, and Annie took a forty-minute group lesson from Coach Knudson three afternoons a week and on Saturdays when the coach wasn't traveling with skaters to competitions. Erica took private lessons with Coach Knudson.

Erica was also a member of the Pine Creek Figure Skating Club, which had separate lockers at the rink and rented ice time for members only to take lessons and practice. That meant that the ice was much less crowded during Erica's lessons.

"Lauren," said the coach. "Your turn."

Lauren skated forward and picked up speed. I can do this, I can do this, she thought. Step, lift . . .

And then she was spinning in the air, weightless and free for just one moment. In the next moment, her skate had landed and she was gliding around on the back outside edge of her foot. She lifted her arms and her chin, imagining that she was in front of the judges.

"Very nice, Lauren," said Coach Knudson. "In fact, you are all coming along very well. I think you'll be in good shape for the North Atlantic Regionals."

Danielle let her breath out in a long sigh. "Well, I *hope* so," she said. "Otherwise, major disaster. Total doom." Danielle reveled in drama. Nothing was ever less than major in her life.

"It's time," said Coach Knudson, looking at her watch. She smiled and nodded at the three girls, then skated over to the entrance to the rink where Erica was waiting for her lesson.

Danielle glided to the edge of the rink and leaned way, way over. She was the tallest of the three of them, with long legs and graceful arms and a good reach. She snagged a water bottle from the seat on the first row and passed it back to Annie. She grabbed a second for Lauren and a third for herself. They all took long drinks.

"Soon we'll be going to the North Atlantic Regionals," said Annie dreamily. "Triple triple toe loop, can you believe it?"

"We've been novices for a whole year," said Danielle. "It'll be a piece of cake."

Lauren and Annie both looked at Danielle. "Okay, *practically* a whole year," said Danielle. "*Probably* a piece of cake."

For the best skaters, the North Atlantic Regionals was the first step on the way to the Eastern Sectionals. From the Sectionals, a maximum of four skaters or couples in each division—ladies', men's, pairs, and ice dancing—could go on to the Novice National Championships. And from there . . .

The world, thought Lauren as she shivered.

This time it wasn't the cold. *The Olympics.*

"Is your costume ready yet for the long program?" Annie asked Danielle.

"Almost. I'm going to look just like Nancy Kerrigan in the 1994 Olympics," Danielle boasted. "Only maybe even more absolutely fabulous." Danielle was tall and graceful like Nancy Kerrigan, it was true. But she had short, wildly curly blond hair, hazel eyes, and a round face, not at all like the Olympic silver medalist's.

"Your costume cost thirteen thousand dollars, like Nancy's would have if the designer hadn't donated it to her?" said Annie in mock surprise.

"No! Of course not. But you know it's being made specially. It's going to have lots and lots of silver on it," Danielle retorted. "*Way* elegant. Wait till you see it. *And* it coordinates with my short program outfit, which, as you know, is pale blue with a blue-and-silver ribbon-striped overskirt."

"Silver is nice. But green's my lucky color," Annie said. Annie's short program costume was sage green and white. After making that momentous decision, she had gone through books and books of patterns with her costume maker before picking out a sleek design with a complicated tucked skirt that would float in a cloud around her as she spun. Now they were debating over the exact color of green for the sleek, V-necked pattern Annie had chosen for her long program competition. "Don't you hate standing still for all those fittings?" Annie asked. "It's the worst."

"It's not *that* bad," said Lauren. Her mother made all her costumes, not a designer or a costume maker, and Lauren didn't mind trying on her costume over and over. It was like shopping, but without spending the money. "But it's true, I would rather be skating."

"Who wouldn't?" asked Danielle. "Or shopping." She flung out her arms. "My second-favorite sport."

"Shopping is not a sport, Danielle," Annie retorted.

"Sure it is," said Danielle. "Like hunting. Only you're hunting clothes, not killing helpless animals."

"Danielle!" Lauren shook her head.

"Anyway, don't forget we'll be out stalking the perfect costume material this weekend."

Danielle and Annie were going with Lauren and Mrs. Wing on Saturday afternoon to a fabric outlet to choose material for Lauren's long program costume. She and her mother had decided to combine two patterns that Lauren had used before, to create a new pattern. But Lauren hadn't been able to find the right material—well, the right not-too-expensive material.

At least the costume for her short program wasn't a problem, Lauren thought. For that, her mother was putting a new pale blue skirt with contrasting midnight-blue trim on the dark blue costume she'd worn before. That helped save money. I'll need new skates soon, though, thought Lauren.

"Shop until you drop!" said Danielle, interrupting the gloomy direction of Lauren's thoughts. She held her water bottle up in the air.

"Skate until you drop, you mean," said Annie. She grabbed Lauren's water bottle and tossed it and her own onto the seat behind the rink wall. Then she punched Danielle on the shoulder. "You're it! You're the duck!"

She swooped away and glided into a sit, one leg extended straight out in front of her. Lauren went after her. Now Danielle would have to tag one of them while she was in the same position, called shoot-the-duck.

They raced around the rink, playing goofy games of tag for the last few minutes of ice time.

Then suddenly Danielle straightened up and stopped so abruptly that Lauren ran right into her. She reeled back. Lauren's left foot went up in the air, and her right foot followed. She crashed to the ice.

"Hey!" she yelled.

But Danielle wasn't even looking at Lauren. She was staring across the ice, her hazel eyes wide, her mouth half open.

"Hey," Lauren said again. "Earth to Danielle. You just made me wipe out here, in case you didn't notice."

Annie slid to a stop beside them. "What happened?"

"I think Danielle forgot how to skate," said

Lauren, as Annie turned and reached down to give Lauren a hand up.

Danielle shook her head. "It's her," she said in an awed voice. She crossed her hands over her heart. "I so totally can't believe my eyes."

"Her, who?" asked Annie, looking over her shoulder.

"Eve Perry," said Danielle.

"Eve Perry?" Annie squeaked. She let go of Lauren's hand, completely forgetting about helping Lauren to her feet. *Thump!* Lauren fell back down on the ice—hard.

"Ow!" she cried.

"You're kidding," Annie said. She clutched Danielle's arm. "Where?"

"There," said Danielle, gesturing with her chin toward the far end of the rink. She had clenched her hands into fists at her side as if she were having trouble preventing herself from pointing.

Lauren, Annie, and Danielle stared. Lauren didn't see anyone at first. Then, as her gaze traveled to the top row, she recognized someone she had only seen in photographs, a small, slight figure wrapped in a bright, taxi-yellow coat.

According to all the articles, Eve Perry's favorite color was bright yellow, which she almost always wore.

In the photographs, Eve Perry was small, and swept her dark hair up into a bun, just as this woman did.

Eve Perry had been a famous skater. She had retired from skating long ago to become an even more famous coach in Washington State.

"Eve Perry," Lauren breathed reverently. What was Eve Perry doing at the Pine Creek Skating Rink? Lauren scrambled to her feet, keeping her eyes fixed on the slight, faraway figure.

At that moment, Eve Perry looked down toward the three girls.

And at that moment, somehow, Lauren lost her balance and crashed back to the ice right in front of practically the most famous coach in the whole wide world.

3

Lauren unwrapped her sandwich and sighed. Peanut butter and double mixed jelly. Today it was grape and apricot. No surprise, since she'd made it herself.

She bit a hole in the exact middle of her sandwich and chewed, thinking depressed thoughts. She swallowed. She leaned her chin on her hand and watched Rebecca Meyers cross the lunchroom toward where Lauren sat at their usual table by the back window. Rebecca didn't even notice when Annie dashed by, until Annie spoke. Beck could sometimes be single-minded, especially when it came to science. They'd just come from science class, which they had together, and from Rebecca's faraway expression, Lauren could tell that Rebecca was still thinking about the migratory patterns of monarch butterflies.

Even though Annie passed Rebecca every day on the way out of the lunchroom, Rebecca was too focused to see her. Annie, who was a year older than Lauren and in the class ahead of her, had a different lunch period. Danielle went to a private school, where she was in the same class as Erica.

Annie waved at Lauren and vanished into a knot of students shoving their way out of the lunchroom door, while Rebecca settled her tray carefully on the table.

As always, chaos ruled the Pine Creek School lunchroom. Shrieks of laughter came from the table of cheerleaders near the front of the lunchroom. Randy Bishop, a tall, thin, restless boy with a fright wig of sandy hair, stood up and bowed. Randy was the class clown. It figured he'd be in the middle of the most noise.

"I can't believe we *ever* thought Randy was cute," and Lauren said, as Randy tucked his hands under his armpits and began to squawk like a chicken.

Rebecca looked up then. She turned in the direction of the loudest laughter and watched with Lauren and most of the lunchroom as Randy produced two carrots and made himself into a vegetable-toothed vampire.

She turned back to Lauren and sat down. "We were *very* young," she said. "First grade was *years* ago."

"True," Lauren said. "But how come we changed, and Randy never did?"

"Because boys take longer to mature," Rebecca said loftily. "It's a scientific fact."

Lauren and Rebecca had become best friends in first grade in part because of Randy. They'd both had a crush on him.

Their competing crushes had erupted into a fight on the playground over which one of them got to choose Randy for her kickball team. They'd started out as enemies, but ended as friends. Now Lauren counted on Rebecca's loyalty and understanding; and Rebecca, an only child, treated Lauren like a sister.

Lauren sighed again, as long and noisily as she could. Even in all the din of the lunchroom, the sigh was *loud*.

Rebecca looked up, startled. "Did you say something?"

"Yes," said Lauren. "I sighed. With despair. Doom. Depression. No big deal. Don't worry. Just doom, depression, and despair."

"Despair," repeated Rebecca. "Oh." She paused, then grinned. "I thought I detected a cloud of gloom in the science class. But I thought it must have been someone else's experiment."

"Ha," said Lauren. "Ha."

"This despair—would it be about ice skating?"

"How did you know?" asked Lauren.

Rebecca gave Lauren her Rebecca look, narrowing her eyes and raising her right eyebrow. "Lauren, how long have we known each other?"

"I talk about other things besides ice skating," protested Lauren.

"Yes, but you don't sigh with . . . doom, depression, and despair over anything else." Rebecca finished her slaw, brushed her bangs from her eyes, and said, "What happened?"

"The worst. I fell and . . ."

"You fall all the time. 'Half of skating is getting up when you fall.' That's what you always say."

Rebecca had a very good memory and was a monster for accuracy. Normally, Lauren appreciated this characteristic in her friend. But not at the moment.

"This was different. Totally different! I fell in front of Eve Perry," Lauren explained. "Like a big, dumb tree, or something."

"You could never look like a big, dumb tree, even falling, and who is Eve Perry?"

"Eve Perry is *the* coach of the universe. The figure skating, like, well, Albert Einstein. Or Marie Curie."

"Oh," said Rebecca. She considered this for a second. "I guess falling in front of Eve Perry is bad?"

"The worst. The absolute worst. I just lay there wishing I were dead. Or wearing a mask. A full-body disguise."

"Then you *would* have been conspicuous,"

said Rebecca. "Dead or in disguise, I can guarantee you'd have been the only one like that in the rink. I bet she didn't even notice you, Lauren. You weren't the only person in the skating rink, were you?"

"No," said Lauren. "Just the only person doing ice dives."

"And even if she did see you fall, she doesn't know who you are," Rebecca went on.

Lauren sighed a third time. "Somehow, you are not cheering me up."

Rebecca divided her turkey dog into sections, as if she were dissecting it. She looked up and smiled at Lauren, the corners of her brown eyes crinkling. "She'll know who you are one day, Lauren. The whole world will."

"You think?"

"I know," said Rebecca. "Scientific fact. You're the gold, Lauren. One day, you and this Perry person will look back and laugh. 'Remember how I did a swan dive on the ice the first time I saw you?' you'll say to her. And she'll say, 'I knew even then it was the swan dive of a champion.'"

"Swan dives are for swimming pools. But thanks, Beck," said Lauren.

Rebecca grinned her lopsided grin. "Anytime," she said. "You want to come over today, after your lesson?"

"No lesson today," said Lauren. "Just practice."

"After practice, then? What you need is a nonskating activity. I'll get my mom to take us to the mall and we can—"

"No shopping," Lauren said. "I'm going shopping on Saturday for material for my skating costume."

"A movie. You know, that one about the cat that goes back in time. We can get pizza afterward."

"That should be okay. I'll call Mom after lunch to make sure," Lauren said.

"Good. We'll pick you up at four-thirty. The movie's at four-fifty," said Rebecca.

"Done deal," agreed Lauren.

"Unless you want to make cookies," Rebecca offered. "For a science project. That'd be fun, too."

Lauren smiled to herself. As much as she liked science, she would never understand Rebecca's passion for it, any more than Rebecca would ever understand how Lauren's idea of fun could be to spend hours doing the same moves over and over on a pair of silver blades on a sheet of ice.

"I like the movie idea better," Lauren said.

"Okay," said Rebecca cheerfully.

At that moment, someone in the lunch line dropped a tray. A cheer swept through the lunchroom, and Randy leaped to his feet again, pretending he was a cheerleader. "Two six eight four!" he shouted. "Drop your lunch on the floor!"

Rebecca rolled her eyes and leaned forward. "Two six eight four, throw Randy out the door," she said.

Lauren started to laugh, and she forgot all about Coach Perry.

4

Lauren fumbled with the key, jammed it into the lock and slammed the kitchen door back. Like the white rabbit in *Alice in Wonderland*, she was late, late, late. Rebecca would be there any minute to pick her up for the movie.

She raced upstairs, dropped her skating bag, and dumped the money out of her piggy bank. She thrust the money into her pocket, and peered out the window. Mrs. Meyers's car was outside. Lauren threw the window up. She pushed up the storm window, too, and leaned perilously out. "I'm coming!" she called.

Rebecca saw Lauren and waved.

The phone began to ring.

Lauren ran back downstairs and snatched it up. It was her mother, reminding her to take the casserole out of the freezer for dinner.

"Right," Lauren gasped. She hung up the phone and took care of the casserole. She hated being late like this. She always forgot something.

What was she forgetting? Money, house keys . . . the casserole was taken care of.

She ran out the back door, being careful to lock it behind her, and dashed to the car.

"Sorry. We're going to be late, and it's my fault," Lauren said. "Practice went a little over."

"No big deal," Rebecca said. "They always show about a million stupid trailers and advertisements anyway."

Reassured, Lauren relaxed a little. "Hi, Mrs. Meyers."

Mrs. Meyers peered over her dark glasses at Lauren. "Hi yourself," she said. "Rebecca's father and I are going to meet you after the movie and have pizza with you. I hope this is acceptable."

"Sure," said Lauren.

"Can we sit at our own table?" Rebecca asked.

"I'm hurt," her mother said. "But I guess I'll live."

"Good," said Rebecca. "'Cause I don't have enough money for pizza."

Lauren grinned. Rebecca and her mother talked like that all the time. Lauren was used to it, but she'd seen the startled looks of other people who weren't. In spite of the fact that she was an only child, Rebecca led a pretty rules-free life that Lauren sometimes envied.

"See you at dinner," Mrs. Meyers said as they got out of the car.

Soon they settled into their seats over a bag of popcorn as the movie trailers were ending.

"Perfect timing," Rebecca said with a sigh of satisfaction. "I'm going to close my eyes during the scary parts. Don't forget to tell me when they're over."

"Beck," Lauren said. "This is a movie about a time-traveling cat. There won't be any scary parts."

"There might be," said Rebecca.

Sure enough, the movie had barely begun before Rebecca had slid down in the seat, squinched her eyes shut, and put her hands over her ears.

The time-traveling cat blasted through the window to other dimension amid a cacophony of sound effects. Lauren grabbed one of Rebecca's arms. "It's okay now," she whispered. "The cat made it."

"Oh, good," Rebecca breathed, sitting up and opening her eyes.

As they left the movie, Lauren said, "Beck, I don't know if you've noticed, but when the stars of movies get in trouble, they always make it out alive. The cat was never in danger."

"I know," said Rebecca. She grinned. "But it's more fun that way."

Lauren shook her head. "You are hopeless."

After a quick tour of the mall, with a stop in the sports shop to look at ice skates, and in the bookstore to check out the latest book in their favorite series, they met Rebecca's parents at the pizza parlor.

Mrs. Meyers challenged them to a game of hangman, and Lauren and Rebecca ended up sitting in a booth with Mr. and Mrs. Meyers after all, eating pizza and scribbling madly on the paper tablecloth with the crayons the pizza parlor provided.

"Salchow?" Rebecca guessed, winning the last game with only the letters "S," "A," and "L" showing. The Salchow was one of the jumps in Lauren's figure skating program.

"Right," Lauren admitted reluctantly.

"How did you know that?" Mr. Meyers asked his daughter.

"Lauren talks about skating all the time," Rebecca said. She gave an exaggerated, long-suffering sigh. "Sometimes I listen."

When Lauren got home, she had almost forgotten about Eve Perry. Rebecca was a true-blue friend and she'd been right—a little quality movie and pizza time had put the whole encounter with the famous coach into perspective.

Plus, thought Lauren happily as she pushed open the kitchen door, almost no homework. Life is good.

Lisa's wail stopped her. "He's gone!" she howled. "He's gone."

"Lisa? Lacey? Mom? I'm home," Lauren said. She hung her key on the rack by the back door and hurried into the family room. Lisa raised her tear-streaked face. "Lutz has run away," she cried.

"Lutz! Lutz! Here, kitty, kitty," Lacey called.

"Lutzzz," Lisa piped up, from her father's shoulder.

"We'll divide up at the corner," Mr. Wing said. "Lacey, you and Bryan go that way. Lisa and I will stay on this street."

"Lauren and I will circle the block in the other direction," Mrs. Wing said.

Lauren didn't say anything. She was busy feeling rotten.

"I'm so sorry," she said again as she and her mother turned up the next street. "It's all my fault. I can't believe I left the window of my room open."

Mrs. Wing patted Lauren's shoulder. "You didn't mean for Lutz to get out, dear. And he can't have gone far. We'll find him."

But they didn't. They searched for another

hour, calling and rattling a box of Lutz's favorite treats. Dogs barked at them, and the shapes of other cats watched them from the steps and windows of houses, but no Lutz.

At last they went home.

"We'll make some signs to put around the neighborhood tomorrow," Mr. Wing said. "We'll find him."

Lisa buried her head in her father's neck as he carried her up to put her to bed.

"He's been on the street before," Lacey said. "He knows how to take care of himself."

"But he's a house cat now," Lauren said. "We never let him out unless we're outside with him. He'll never find his way home."

Just like the cat in the movie, Lutz had gone out the window—and disappeared.

5

Lauren dipped into a layback spin, holding her position as tightly as possible. If she did it right, she'd be a blur of color and motion at center ice. This move was the finale of her program for the competition in two weeks. The Pine Creek skating rink hosted a competition every fall. The program Lauren was practicing was a less complicated version of the program she was working on for the Regionals. By the time of the Regionals, she hoped to be able to hold her spin much longer, and to be certain of her double Salchow–double toe loop combination jumps.

But not now. One spin at a time, she thought, raising her arms upward. She lost her balance and wobbled and had to lower her arms abruptly. She jammed her toe pick into the ice and stepped out heavily from the spin.

"Keep your center of balance low," Coach Knudson said. "And stay focused."

How can I stay focused? Lauren thought. Lutz is gone.

She tried to imagine Lutz sliding slyly out the window. He would have jumped to the roof of the garage and then down, maybe, on the the lids of the garbage cans lined up along one side.

But then where would he have gone? Had a barking dog scared him and made him run for his life? Had he raced into the street and not seen an oncoming car and . . .

No. Lauren put the thought out of her head. She'd skip practice today, too. She'd go home after her lesson and look some more. Her father had said he would make signs for them to put up around the neighborhood. They would offer a reward. Lutz would be found. Or maybe he'd just mysteriously reappear.

"Lauren?"

Coach Knudson was waiting. Willing herself

to concentrate, Lauren skated away to begin the crossover strokes into her spin again.

But it was no use. This time she didn't even make it. She fell. Just like that.

"I don't believe this," she muttered.

"Concentrate, Lauren," Coach Knudson said. Danielle gave Lauren a sympathetic look. Lauren had told Danielle and Annie about Lutz before the lesson. They knew how worried she was.

"I am concentrating," Lauren said. She got up. She was concentrating—just not on skating.

Meanwhile, nearby, Annie did her double toe loop over and over.

Finally, Coach Knudson looked at her watch. "Bring it in," she said, motioning to her three students. "And let's talk for a minute."

Lauren, Annie, and Danielle gathered around Coach Knudson.

"I had a very interesting visitor a few days ago," Coach Knudson began.

Eve Perry, Lauren thought, remembering the familiar figure they'd seen high above the rink two days before. She felt a stab of nervousness in her stomach, as if she was about to skate onto center ice at a competition.

"She's someone you all might know," Coach Knudson went on. "A coach. Eve Perry."

"It *was* her," squeaked Annie. "I knew it!"

Coach Knudson looked at Annie in surprise.

"We saw her, watching the skaters, right after practice on Monday," Danielle explained.

"Ah," said Coach Knudson.

"Why was she here?" Lauren asked.

"The Silver Springs Figure Skating Club just completed a brand-new rink south of here, just outside of Saratoga," said Coach Knudson. "Eve has joined the club as the coach."

"That's just an hour away." Danielle said reverently.

Annie hugged herself. "Wow! Maybe we'll get to meet her. I mean, will we, Coach?"

"I think I can promise you will," said Coach Knudson. "Eve and I go way back. We've known each other since I was a novice." Coach Knudson had skated competitively for many years, earning a National Juniors title, a National Seniors title, and a silver medal at the

World Championships before retiring.

Eve Perry had won her share of titles, too, long before Coach Knudson. But her legendary skill as a coach was her claim to fame. "Queen Midas of Figure Skating Coaches" one newspaper article had dubbed her, because so many of her skaters had won gold medals.

"Did Coach Perry . . . was she *your* coach?" Lauren blurted out.

"No. But she made suggestions to me and my coach, and we were both grateful. Some people find Eve difficult. But that's only because she has never let anyone get away with less than their best. 'Better than your best, that's the way to win,' she used to say. But you'll see. Now, let's do a few stretches to cool down."

Lauren pulled on her leg warmers and began to stretch, forcing herself to move slowly although her thoughts were racing.

Putting one foot on the railing, Lauren stretched her legs, her thoughts chasing each other around and around. What if Coach Perry showed up during a lesson? Maybe she would nod toward Lauren and whisper a few words of advice for Lauren in Coach Knudson's ear.

She straightened up. "I have to go," she said.

To her surprise, Annie and Danielle didn't skate away to begin their practice. They stepped out of the rink and began to remove their skates.

"What are you doing?" Lauren asked.

"Going on a Lutz hunt," Annie said.

"But what about practice?"

Danielle shrugged. "We can practice another time. Right now, this is more important."

Lauren felt a rush of gratitude. Maybe Danielle and Annie would have better luck in finding Lutz. "Thank you," she said.

"Any time," said Annie.

6

Rebecca was sitting at Lauren's kitchen table with Lacey when Lauren, Annie, and Danielle walked in.

"Beck," said Lauren. "What are you doing here?"

"Waiting for you. I'm going to help you look for Lutz. After all, I'm a cat expert."

"And Lutz knows you, too," said Annie. She and Danielle knew the whole story of how Rebecca and Lauren had rescued the big gray cat. That Rebecca had helped Lauren nurse Lutz back to health after he'd been saved from life as a street kitten.

At that moment, Bryan came into the kitchen

with a big envelope under one arm. "Here they are," he said. "The Lutz 'Wanted' posters. Dad had them made today. I just picked them up from the restaurant."

He pulled a sheet of paper out of the envelope and held it up. At the top of the poster were the words LOST CAT and REWARD in big letters. Beneath that was a picture of Lutz. Below Lutz's picture was his description with the time, date, and place he'd been lost, and the Wings' home phone number, as well as the phone number at the restaurant.

Rebecca inspected the poster with a critical eye, then nodded. "Good work," she said. "Did he have on a collar and ID tag?"

"No," said Mrs. Wing, coming into the kitchen with Lisa trailing after her. "He was an indoor cat."

"Doesn't matter," Rebecca said crisply. "You never know when a cat will get out, like now."

Mrs. Wing nodded. "Good point. When we get him back, he'll get a collar and tag."

When we get him back, Lauren thought, and felt more hopeful than she had. Then she thought, but what if we don't? But there was no time to think about that now.

Rebecca took brisk, efficient charge of the operation. In what seemed like no time, they'd divided up and were scattered throughout the neighborhood, looking for Lutz and putting his picture up everywhere they could.

When they quit, signs for Lutz could be seen on posts and trees all over the neighborhood.

"Thanks, guys," she said.

"If he hasn't come back, we'll do some more this weekend," Annie offered.

"I'll put this up at my school," Danielle said, tucking one of the signs into her skating bag.

"Don't worry. We'll find him," said Rebecca.

And seeing the determined look on the faces of her three friends, Lauren began to really believe that they might after all.

"Achoo! AAAAA-*choo*! I'm about to *expire* and *explode* from this smell!" cried Danielle.

Lauren wrinkled her nose and squinted her eyes against the sharp smell of the stacks and stacks of material piled on table after table, aisle after aisle. It was Saturday morning, and Mrs. Wing had driven Lauren, Danielle, and Annie to an enormous fabric warehouse. They'd already looked in stores closer to home (where, at Annie's suggestion, they'd put up signs for Lutz), but nothing that the Wings could afford looked right for the pattern Lauren had chosen for her long program costume.

Danielle had wandered away to the drawers of buttons and racks of trim. She held up a length of rickrack. "This would be cool on a costume," she said. "Like a uniform, you know? But cooler. With a hat and a feather."

"A hat! No way," said Annie. "With my luck, the hat would fall over my eyes."

"What about red?" Mrs. Wing suggested, shifting several bolts to unroll a length of jersey.

Lauren inspected the cardinal-colored stretch of material and said, "Maybe."

"Look at this!" Danielle pointed. "Hawaiian prints. These would look *great*. I'm going to ask for a sample to show my mom."

"Not for me," said Lauren.

"Black is very sophisticated," suggested Annie.

Lauren wrinkled her nose. "I'd look like a crow."

They wandered the aisles. Gold and silver, prints and checks, gingham and pinstripes swirled by. Lauren ran her hand along butter-soft velvets and tissue-thin muslins, but nothing seemed right.

Then, just as Lauren was about to give up, she saw the swirl of white lace buried beneath a jumbled heap of leftover bolts of fabric on a table in the back. Lace was often expensive. But this was on a remnant table, and it had been marked down. She touched it gently. The price was right, but what could she do with it?

"It's beautiful," said Annie.

"There's not very much left, though," Danielle pointed out.

"I know," said Lauren. She looked up at her mother.

"A sash and a skirt might just be possible," said Mrs. Wing, unfurling the lace and measuring it with an expert eye. "Yes. There's enough material for that. If we put it over a fitted leotard with long sleeves, it might make a lovely costume."

"Yellow," said Lauren, suddenly, thinking for

no reason at all of Eve Perry. "Like daffodils in the spring."

Mrs. Wing studied Lauren thoughtfully. "Yes," she said. "And we can tuck a silk daffodil into your hair. Maybe with a bit of the same lace."

"Elegant," said Annie.

"Yes," said Lauren, pleased. "Elegant."

"Like a daffodil and Queen Anne's lace in spring, see?" Lauren said, holding up a sketch of the costume her mother had made.

Rebecca looked up from her frowning at the plate of hockey-puck-hard cookies on the kitchen table. "Daffodils grow from bulbs in the early spring," she said. "Queen Anne's lace—a weed related to the carrot—is a summer flower."

"Whatever," said Lauren, smiling.

"Uh-huh," said Beck. She picked up a cookie and tapped it on the table. "Long, slow baking definitely makes these into little rocks."

"That's what you wanted, isn't it?" Lauren sniffed. Not only were the cookies the density of cement, they also smelled like garlic. Rebecca

was making dog cookies for the family dachs-
hunds, Alice and Clyde.

One of the seven cats that also shared the
Meyerses' house squeezed through the cat door
and sat down at Lauren's feet.

"Bootsie," Lauren said, leaning over to pick
him up.

He went limp as Lauren lifted him and began
to purr loudly. Bootsie was black with four white
paws, a white patch over one eye, and one ear
missing. He'd been hit by a car and left with a
veterinarian, who had called the Meyerses to see
if they would nurse another cat back to health.

The answer, of course, had been yes.

Lauren felt a lump in her throat as she
thought about Lutz. Quickly, she slid Bootsie
out of her lap.

"He'll be back," said Rebecca, reading
Lauren's thoughts.

Lauren folded the sketch into her notebook
without answering and picked up one of the
cookies. "What's in these dog biscuits? Besides
garlic, I mean."

"Carrots. Applesauce. Wheat germ. Flour,"

said Rebecca, accepting the change of subject without comment. Lutz had been missing for almost a week, and even Rebecca found it hard to argue that he was just out exploring.

She went on, "I was going to put in some raisins, but I couldn't find any."

"Garlic raisin cookies?" said Lauren. "Ugh."

"That's not what Alice and Clyde say. Do you, guys?"

Both dogs began to bark.

"Lutz wouldn't touch those cookies," Lauren said. "I don't even think my brother would, and he's pretty much a vacuum cleaner when it comes to food."

"I don't know about Bryan, but cats have different rules from dogs. Besides, garlic helps keep fleas away."

"I can see why. Garlic dog-breath would kill more than fleas," Lauren said. She paused, then said, "So . . . are you going to come to the Pine Creek Competition this Saturday?"

"You know I will," said Rebecca. She looked up and grinned and proved that she'd been listening all along. "I sure will . . . daffodil."

7

I don't feel like a daffodil today, thought Lauren. I feel like a pressed flower.

She jumped back as a large woman with an armful of clothing swept by, followed by twin girls drooping under the weight of bulging duffel bags.

"Hey," protested Annie. "Watch it."

"Stand still, Annie," said Moira McGrath, Annie's sister. She was a seventeen-year-old version of Annie, with Annie's dark hair and flashing eyes.

Moira wasn't a figure skater anymore, but she still went to most of Annie's competitions, helping out and bossing Annie around.

The locker room at the Pine Creek Skating Rink was crammed with competitors in the annual Competition. With the competitors came coaches, parents, siblings, and friends.

Lauren spotted a familiar knot of curly blond hair bobbing along in the sea of people. "Danielle!" she called, waving her arm. "Over here!"

Danielle charged up, trailed by her mother. Dropping to the bench in front of the lockers, Danielle clutched her throat and said, "I thought I was going to get totally trampled!"

Mrs. Kurowicki smiled. "I don't think you were in any danger, Danielle. Hi, everybody."

"Did you save us a locker?" Danielle asked.

"Right here next to Annie's and mine," said Lauren. Annie had pulled on her jeans. "I have to go to the bathroom."

"*Don't* talk about it," Danielle pleaded. "I don't want to put my costume on and have to take it off again."

"But you will," said Lauren wisely. Danielle was famous at the Pine Creek rink for last-minute dashes to the bathroom before she was scheduled to go out onto the ice.

Maybe it keeps her from thinking about her program and being so nervous, Lauren thought.

"You already have your costume on," Danielle said in an accusing voice.

"I just put it on," said Lauren. "Mom went to get Lisa and Lacey so they could wish me luck."

Mrs. Kurowicki opened the locker and hung Danielle's clothing bag over the door. She unzipped the bag and Lauren felt a stab of envy at the sleek costume inside. Even for small competitions, Danielle had beautiful new costumes. Although this wasn't the striking silver costume she had planned for the North Atlantic Regionals, it was a standout: a long slash of lavender, with insets of dark purple in the skirt, at the neck, and in the flowing sleeves. The costume was made to accentuate Danielle's long, tall build.

Feeling self-conscious, Lauren smoothed the skirt of her soft blue outfit for her short program. Her mother had stitched new navy and gold braid on it, and twined gold braid in the French knot of Lauren's hair, but Lauren suddenly felt lumpy and dowdy.

As if reading Lauren's thoughts, Danielle looked up. "You look great, Lauren. That braid is extra super."

"Thanks," said Lauren. "You look pretty decent yourself." Costumes are important, she reminded herself, but they're not the most important part of skating. The most important part is how you skate.

Moira finished tacking down the ruffle on Annie's costume and bit the thread. "That should do it," she said.

Something hit Lauren from behind, right above her knees. She twisted and looked down at Lisa. "You look beautiful," Lisa said, her face shining with admiration.

Lauren laughed. "You say that about every costume I have."

"That's because they're all beautiful," Lisa answered solemnly.

"She's right, too," said Rebecca.

Lauren saw her mother smile, looking pleased.

"Beck! Hi. You did make it!" Lauren said.

Rebecca looked surprised. "Of course I did. I told you I would, didn't I? To cheer for the best skater in Pine Creek."

"Who's the best skater?" demanded Danielle in a muffled voice from inside her costume, which was halfway down over her head. "Are you talking about Lauren, Annie—or me?"

"Okay, the *three* best skaters in Pine Creek," Rebecca said.

Mrs. Wing sat down on the bench and pulled Lisa onto her lap to keep her out of the way. Danielle wiggled on the bench as Mrs. Kurowicki began to apply her makeup. Annie returned from the bathroom and sat patiently as Moira applied eyeliner, eyebrow pencil, and all kinds of makeup and color.

"How come you don't wear makeup, too?" Lisa asked Lauren.

"Lauren doesn't need to wear makeup yet," said Mrs. Wing.

Lauren flashed Danielle and Annie an embarrassed look as she sat down on the bench. Her parents thought she was too young to wear the layers of makeup most girls wore. It was kind of embarrassing that her parents treated her like a little kid, but deep down she didn't mind so much about not being able to wear makeup. With all the blush and shadow and mascara and liner, many of the girls looked like clowns.

"Time to go," Mrs. Wing said to Lisa. She bent forward and kissed Lauren lightly on the cheek. "Do your best," she said.

"I will," Lauren promised. She remembered what Coach Knudson had said and added, to herself, *Better than my best.*

8

"Well, melt the ice and stop the show," said Danielle. She clapped her hand to her cheek. Lauren noticed that Danielle had on lavender fingernail polish to match her costume. "Look." Her voice had dropped to a dramatic whisper.

The three girls peered around the edge of the waiting area out into the rink. "What? *What*?" Annie demanded. "If you're trying to psych me out, Danielle, I promise I'll . . ."

"I wouldn't do that!" Danielle protested.

Annie gave Danielle a skeptical sideways look. "I think you tried to psych me out with that short program you just skated."

"It was only practically perfect. No big deal," Danielle said airily. For once, she wasn't exaggerating.

Annie and Lauren were still waiting their turn on the ice.

"Danielle," Lauren warned.

"You're in triple-triple-Axel–double-death-spiral danger," Annie added. "What are we supposed to be looking at?"

"Okay, okay." Danielle leaned forward and whispered, *"She's here."*

"Who?" asked Annie.

"Who's here?" asked Lauren at the same time. But she knew the answer before Danielle told them.

"Eve Perry. Straight across the rink. See?"

"Where? I don't see her." Annie scanned the stands.

"It's true," Lauren said, her heart lurching. "Danielle's telling the truth. Third row up over there. Middle of the bleachers."

Lauren looked up. She wondered why she hadn't noticed Eve Perry sooner. How long had the coach been there?

"Do you think she saw me skate?" Danielle said. "I hope so."

"Great. Thanks, Danielle! Now *I* have to skate knowing *she's* up there."

Lauren felt sick to her stomach.

What if she couldn't do her double–double combination in her long program? Maybe she shouldn't try such a hard jump in her long program.

But how sure would she ever be? If she didn't try it now, when would she? The Regionals weren't far away, and she had to know if she could do this program. Now was the time to make mistakes.

No, she told herself fiercely. Don't think about making mistakes.

She turned and clomped back to a bench, sat down, and stared at her skates, willing her mind to empty, her body to stay relaxed, her heart not to race.

And willing herself, most of all, not to think about Eve Perry sitting up in the stands of the Pine Creek Skating Rink.

"Good luck, Annie," Lauren heard Danielle

say. She saw Annie taking off her blade guards at the edge of the rink. Coach Knudson stood next to Annie, talking softly. Lauren jumped up and hurried over. "Go for the sixes," she said.

Annie nodded, her face pale. Then she pasted a smile on her face as her name was called.

Lauren watched, one part of her cheering her friend on, the other part judging her performance. Annie's movements were not as graceful as they could have been. She performed each required element of the short program with accuracy, but without real expression. The smile on her face was the smile of a skater thinking about her next move.

When she finished, people cheered. And this time the smile on Annie's face was genuine. She looked relieved. But Lauren could see the tenseness in Annie's shoulders, the heaviness with which she skated off the ice.

Annie knew her scores wouldn't be good.

"I blew it," she moaned, bending to slip her blade guards on.

"You did not!" said Lauren.

"You've done better," Coach Knudson said.

"And you can do better. Focus on what you did right."

'Annie's chin came up. "You're right. This is only the beginning. Just the short program." Annie smiled hugely, turned, and waved at her family as if she'd just scored all sixes.

Lauren felt a flash of admiration for Annie. She knew how hard that had to be.

Coach Knudson patted Annie's shoulder. "Good work," she said. "Now stay hydrated and get changed for the long program."

"Okay," said Annie, looking more cheerful.

"Good idea. And rest. The long program competition will be sooner than you think."

My short program is after the next skater, Lauren realized. She turned away and began to stretch gently, trying to empty her mind of all the worries that began to race through it.

She heard the other skater's music come to an end. She took a deep breath and was about to do one last stretch when she sensed someone behind her. Lauren looked over her shoulder.

Erica stood there, her blue eyes cold and measuring. "Your skating boots could use another coat of polish," she said. "They're awfully scuffed."

In spite of herself, Lauren glanced down at her skates. They were as polished as she could make them, gleaming, soft. Erica was just being nasty—as usual.

"Thank you, Erica," said Lauren. She turned her back on Erica and extended her leg to stretch the hamstring.

"I hope you did a better job sharpening your blades than you did with the polish," Erica persisted. "Judges hate sloppy boots almost as much as they hate sloppy programs."

Lauren ignored Erica. Part of Lauren wanted to turn around and be as nasty back to Erica as Erica was being to her. But if she did that, Lauren would wreck her concentration for sure.

Lauren held her stretch. The music stopped. She heard the ripples of applause.

Erica didn't move.

Lauren didn't move.

At last, Erica said, "Too bad about your cat."

Lauren turned. "What?"

"I saw the sign at my school," Erica said.

"Oh," said Lauren.

"You're probably never going to find him," Erica said. "Lost cats usually just disappear."

How could Erica be so mean? Lauren stared at her without answering. At last Erica shrugged. "Good luck," she said. "You'll need it."

Lauren watched Erica walk away, feeling numb. I will not let her psych me out, Lauren thought. *I won't.* Her gaze dropped to her skates. She bent and ran her thumb along an almost invisible smudge near the inside heel of her right skate boot. My skates look fine, she told herself.

Coach Knudson appeared and said, "Lauren, you're up."

With heavy hands, Lauren removed her guards and handed them to Coach Knudson. She stepped onto the ice. Her feet felt like lumps of lead. The whole world had slowed down—except her heart, which had begun to sledgehammer against her ribs.

She didn't remember how she got to center ice. But suddenly she was there. She struck her pose, raised her arms. Smile, she told herself, and she did.

The music began.

Lauren pushed off in a long glide. The swirl of her skating skirt made her feel giddy for a moment and then she was pushing off with her left foot and rotating counterclockwise in the air. She landed and realized she had completed her first required jump.

Her smile grew broader. Down the rink she swooped, and back, doing each required move. Step, stroke, spiral—the ice spun away beneath her. How quickly it went! Suddenly she was spinning, spinning, spinning, then slowing.

The music stopped. This time, her smile wasn't forced.

Nor was Coach Knudson's. She applauded as Lauren skated toward her. "That was excellent," she said. "Your start was a little tentative, but then you owned the ice. You nailed every move and your footwork was nice and crisp."

"I felt it," said Lauren. She looked up past Coach Knudson and saw her family and Rebecca rise and fall in a miniversion of the "wave." It was so corny that Lauren had to laugh. Then her eyes traveled further.

Coach Perry was still there, motionless amid all the noise and activity. She was wearing dark glasses and her expression was unreadable.

Seeing Coach Perry, Lauren almost didn't care what her scores would be. More than anything, she wanted to ask Eve Perry, "What did you think? How did I do?"

"Awesome," said Danielle, rushing forward as Lauren pulled on her jacket. "Even if you did beat me, it was awesome."

"You could win," said Annie. "You could really win, Lauren."

"Maybe," said Lauren. She linked one arm through Annie's and the other through Danielle's. As they walked into the locker room, Erica slammed her locker and turned.

"Congratulations, Lauren," Erica said, her voice sweet.

Lauren was surprised. "Thank you," she said.

Coach Knudson's voice came from behind Lauren. "Congratulations are in order for everybody. But this competition is not over yet."

9

As the music for Lauren's long program began, she swept one arm up into a graceful arc over her head and extended the other, fingers together, thumb tucked under. She held the pose for a long moment, then pushed off into a long curve of backward crossovers. Her skates skimmed the ice, tracing a sharp, clean edge. Tracing her pattern, she took two long strokes, then went into her combination spin, concentrating on changing feet smoothly in midspin without losing her momentum.

Then she was off again. Double Salchow–double toe loop. Flying camel. After this spin, she skated off strongly and lifted off, this time into a double Axel, and again, she nailed her jump.

She threw her arms out exuberantly and went into a layback spin, making herself a blur of motion and color. She felt wonderful. She could do anything. She could fly.

And she flew toward the end of her long program, feeling powerful and beautiful and as if she ruled the ice. The final jump started perfectly.

And then she fell to earth—or rather, to the ice. Landing, she felt herself swing out wide. She tried to hold on to her jump, but couldn't.

The blur of faces in the audience swung dizzily around her as the ice came up to meet her. Her other foot went down, and a collective groan went up from the crowd. Then Lauren's hand touched the ice.

Automatic two-point deduction, she thought. She clenched her teeth. Anger and the feeling of failure surged through her. She wanted to give up, to quit.

And then a small voice cried out from the hush, "Lauren! Lauren!"

Lisa.

The anger and misery in Lauren gave her the energy to pull herself upright before she could fall completely. Now the ice was her enemy. She tensed her body for the fight.

I won't give up, she thought and smiled as if she was having the most fun she had ever had in her life. She skated away from the broken jump and glided into the final spin of her program as if someone else, not Lauren Wing, had fallen.

She finished right in time with the music.

At least that's something, she thought, and held up both hands and tilted her head as she had practiced so often, remembering, still, to smile.

Nor did she forget to keep smiling as she skated toward Coach Knudson.

I will not cry, I will not cry, I will not cry, she thought, putting both hands into her coach's hands and letting the coach help her off the ice.

She didn't look up for her family. She didn't look for the yellow coat of Coach Perry.

"Lauren! Lauren!" It was Bryan, leaning over at the end of the bench. "Catch!"

Automatically, her hands went up. She caught a bouquet of daffodils.

She gave her head a little shake, and lifted the daffodils to her face to hide her suddenly trembling lips.

Coach Knudson said, "Lauren, you skated a difficult program," she said. "And you pulled off most of it."

"Most of it," said Lauren softly.

"You did well," her coach insisted.

But Lauren barely heard her. "When I stayed on my feet, maybe," she answered bitterly. She wanted to go to the locker room and cry. She wanted a chance to skate the program over.

"You kept skating," said Coach Knudson. "You looked good. Only after you fell did you tighten up. But you kept going. I've seen much worse skating after similar falls." And then she said what Lauren knew she'd say: "It's not falling, it's getting up that counts."

Lauren couldn't be comforted. Winning

counts too, she thought. And today, I'm not a winner.

It was Danielle who brought the news to Lauren and Annie in the locker room.

"Come on, come on!" she cried. "The last skater is almost through. They'll be announcing who won."

Annie's face was red with the struggle to close her locker on the gear that crammed it, and, Lauren suspected, with the effort of not crying herself. Annie's fatal toe loop weakness had caught up with her, and a wobble had turned into a full backside sprawl. Lauren and Danielle had both been watching, had seen the flash of anger in Annie's eyes as she went down.

"Uh-oh," said Danielle, as the anger flamed Annie's cheeks. Sometimes, Annie's temper made her jumps higher, made her spins into sizzling blurs, made her do her very best.

But at other times, like now, Annie's temper got the better of her.

They watched in sympathetic silence while Annie got to her feet. She dug her toe pick viciously into the ice and pushed off.

"I'm surprised she's not melting it," Lauren murmured, watching the searing, harsh edges Annie carved on the ice. She kept her lips pressed tightly together, refusing to smile. She would complete her program, but she wasn't going to pretend. She finished with her fists clenched defiantly.

She had hardly spoken since.

"Danielle, we both fell," said Lauren, when Annie didn't answer.

"In case you didn't notice," Annie added, in a choked voice.

"I know, I know," said Danielle. "But you should be there. Someone might be surprised at how well she did."

"You're right," Annie admitted. "We're bad sports if we aren't there, to applaud for the people who won."

"Even if some of the people aren't quite human," said Danielle. She didn't have to say Erica's name.

Annie managed a tight smile. She looked at Lauren. "I will if you will," she said.

Lauren slammed her locker. "Let's go," she said.

Coach Knudson was sitting on a lower bleacher at the edge of the ice reserved for the skaters and coaches. Lauren's steps slowed as she saw Erica sitting next to the coach.

But before she could turn away, Coach Knudson saw them and motioned them over. "Sit, sit," she said. "Thank you, Danielle, for getting Lauren and Annie."

Danielle said, "And congratulations, Lauren!"

"What?" said Lauren.

"You placed third," Coach Knudson said.

"Me?" asked Lauren. "But Danielle's the one who didn't fall."

"You lucked out," said Erica. "The other programs were even worse than yours with a fall in it." She looked from Lauren to Annie to Danielle.

"Erica," said Coach Knudson.

"I came in first," Erica said.

"Third," said Annie, ignoring Erica. "Oh, Lauren, that's great!"

"But . . ." Lauren glanced at Danielle.

"Fifth," said Danielle. She shrugged. "You earned it, Lauren. Your long program was way tougher than mine."

"Congratulations!" Annie's pleasure in Lauren's and Danielle's success was genuine. "I'm really proud of you guys."

Erica's eyes sparkled maliciously. "Thank you, Annie," she cooed. "That's really nice, especially from someone who finished last."

"That's enough, Erica," said Coach Knudson, sharply.

Surprisingly, Annie didn't lose her temper. It was as if she had run out of temper to lose that day. She rolled her eyes and sat down on the bench between Danielle and Lauren as the announcer began to read the results.

"Congratulations to you all," said the judge, stepping back after she handed Lauren her third-place medal.

People applauded. Cameras flashed.

"Yay, LAUREN!" a voice boomed, and Lauren smiled at her family, where Bryan had jumped up to lead the cheers. I came in third, she told herself. I got back up, and I came in third. Next time, I won't fall. She didn't glance at Erica, but in her mind, Lauren sent Erica toppling to the ice—and to the bottom of the competition.

Smiling, Lauren skated off the ice to where Danielle, Annie, and Coach Knudson waited, applauding.

She turned and waved at her family.

She bent to put on her blade guards. She straightened.

And then, just above Coach Knudson's right shoulder in the bleachers above, Lauren saw the now-familiar figure in a yellow jacket.

10

Lauren stared. As she watched, the dark glasses turned in her direction.

Was Eve Perry looking at Lauren?

Beside her, Erica stepped off the ice and waved vigorously—right at Eve Perry. "I think Coach Perry was here scouting, don't you?" Erica asked.

"Coach Knudson probably invited her." Lauren knew that it wasn't ethical for one coach to try to get a skater away from another coach. But she also knew that it happened sometimes.

Was Eve Perry that kind of coach?

"I think she'll probably want me to skate for her now," Erica said.

"Have you—have you talked to her?" Lauren managed to ask.

"No. Not yet," said Erica. She cut ahead of Lauren, pushing open the locker room door. She looked over her shoulder and added, "But when I do, you'll be one of the first to know. I promise."

The door swung shut in Lauren's face. She stared at it blankly. Erica and Eve Perry?

But Erica *had* come in first. She was a good skater. She was almost as beautiful on the ice as she was nasty off it.

Lauren sighed and pushed her way into the locker room.

The rows of lockers were less crammed with people, and the atmosphere was noticeably calmer. Heads turned, and a knot of people parted as Lauren approached her locker.

"Hey, Lauren, look," said Annie. "It's Team Wing."

Sure enough, Mrs. Wing, Lacey, Lisa, and Rebecca were standing by Lauren's locker. Lisa tugged loose from Lacey's grasp and ran up to Lauren to touch the small bronze medal on the red ribbon around Lauren's neck. "Can I try it on?" she asked. "Please? Can I?"

"May I," Lauren said, flashing a grin at her mother. "Sure. Here." She lifted the medal from around her neck and put it over her youngest sister's head.

Lisa gave a squeal of delight. "Look, Lacey!" she said. "I have Lauren's medal. She gave it to me!"

Feeling suddenly tired, Lauren buried her face in her mother's shoulder. "I'm proud of you," said her mother. "You hung in there."

She didn't say congratulations, and Lauren was grateful. She braced herself as Rebecca came forward and said, "Congratulations, Lauren." Then she smiled wryly as Rebecca leaned over and cuffed Lauren on the shoulder and added, "For getting up."

Mrs. Kurowicki patted Lauren's shoulder. "You girls are a wonder," she said.

"See you at practice," Danielle said, following her mother out of the locker room.

"See you later, alligator," Annie said.

"In a while, crocodile," Lisa piped up. And

then Annie and Moira were gone, too.

Mrs. Wing took charge of Lauren's costumes. Lacey hoisted the skate bag.

"I'll take care of the medal for you, okay?" asked Lisa importantly.

"Thank you, Lisa," Lauren said.

A skater traffic jam blocked the locker room entrance for a moment. When Lauren slid out, she saw her mother talking to Coach Knudson. They turned as Lauren and Rebecca walked up.

"Could I speak to you for a minute, Lauren?" Coach Knudson asked.

Lauren looked at her mother. Mrs. Wing nodded. "We'll meet you at the car," she said.

"I'll wait out by the water fountain," Rebecca said, nodding down the hall.

"Okay," said Lauren. She studied her coach's face. Was something wrong? But Coach Knudson didn't look unhappy or angry. If anything, she looked pleased.

Lauren followed Coach Knudson down the hall. Coach Knudson pushed open a door and led the way into a small room. In a straight-backed chair at the head of the table sat a small, sturdy woman in a yellow jacket with a blazing yellow-and-red scarf knotted at her throat.

Lauren stopped in her tracks. "It's you!" she exclaimed. Then she clapped her hand over her mouth.

Stepping aside, Coach Knudson put one hand lightly on Lauren's shoulder. "Lauren Wing, this is Eve Perry. Eve, this is Lauren Wing, about whom I was telling you."

Coach Perry stood up and strode around the table. She put out her hand. "How do you do, Lauren?"

"Ah, fine. I mean, yes, I'm fine, thanks," Lauren stammered. "How are you?"

Talk about putting my skate in my mouth, thought Lauren. Could I sound any dumber? She tried again. "I'm glad to meet you, Coach Perry."

"Call me Eve," the woman said. Her voice held the faint trace of an accent.

"I couldn't do that," Lauren said, and felt even dumber.

One corner of Eve's mouth twitched. Was that a smile?

Lauren groped for a chair and sat down, never taking her gaze off Eve Perry. Up close, the famous coach had a deeply tanned and lined face.

She wore her silver-streaked dark hair in a French knot today. She'd pushed her dark glasses up, and her eyes were so dark they seemed black. They snapped with energy.

Coach Knudson sat down next to Lauren and Eve Perry resumed her seat in the straight-backed chair, her spine as erect as the chair back. She folded her hands, with short blunt nails and bright polish, on the table in front of her.

"Your coach has told me a great deal about you," Eve began. "And I don't think she exaggerated. It's never been a habit of hers."

Lauren sensed that Coach Knudson was smiling.

Eve went on, "Based on your coach's recommendation, and what I've scouted, I'd like to make you an offer I hope you will not refuse: I'd like to offer you a sponsored membership into the Silver Springs Skating Club, and I'd like to coach you."

Lauren blinked. "What?" she said.

"At Silver Springs sponsorship means your own locker, entry fees in the club-sponsored skating events, the use of the ice during membership time. You'll be responsible for paying for lessons and free ice time. I understand Jenna has spoken to your parents, and they say that if this can be worked out, the only time they can assure me that you can get to lessons consistently is six A.M. This is acceptable to me."

Lauren swallowed hard. "Oh," she said.

"I'll want to meet with your parents. But first, I want you to think it over. Talk it over with Jenna and with your family." Eve Perry stood up. "I'll look forward to your decision. I hope we can work together."

Hardly knowing what she was doing, Lauren stood up, too. Eve held out her hand again, and Lauren shook it automatically.

"I'll talk to you later, Jenna," Eve Perry said to Coach Knudson. With a nod and another quirk of her mouth, she was gone.

Lauren sank back into her chair. She put her hand to her chest in a Danielle move. "I don't believe it," she said. "I don't believe it."

"Eve doesn't joke about skating," Coach Knudson said, her voice amused.

Lauren looked up at her coach. "But what about you?" she asked.

"Eve's not recruiting you out from under my nose, if that's what you're thinking," Coach Knudson said. "I'm the one who suggested she take a look at you. She can teach you things that I can't. I'm a good teacher, Lauren. But I think Eve Perry would be better for you."

"Oh," said Lauren, in a small voice.

Lauren nodded and stood up. Dazed, she followed her coach back down the hall.

"I've already spoken to your mother. I think you should talk to your family and then we should meet together. How does that sound?"

"Fine," Lauren said. She was having trouble thinking. And talking. Her mind was circling faster than any spin she'd ever achieved on ice.

Rebecca waved and started toward them.

"What's going on?" Rebecca asked as Coach Knudson left. "What did your coach want?"

Lauren hesitated. But she wasn't ready to tell

anyone what had happened. Not yet.

She shrugged. "She just wanted to talk about some new training plans."

The answer seemed to satisfy Rebecca. "Oh," she said. "Listen, let's ask if you can sleep over tonight. We'll order pizza and watch science fiction movies. Like that old movie *The Mummy*."

Lauren couldn't help but laugh. "That's not science fiction, Beck. That's horror."

"Mummies are real," Rebecca argued. "That's science. The fiction part is that they come back to life and walk around. . . ."

But Lauren had stopped listening. All she could hear was Eve Perry's voice. "I hope we can work together," she'd said.

If that comes true, thought Lauren, it won't be horror or science fiction. It will be a fairy tale.

11

Mr. Wing looked from Lauren to Coach Knudson and back. The room was silent for a moment. It was late, almost dinnertime, on the following afternoon, and Coach Knudson had just settled down at the kitchen table with Lauren's parents and Lauren. They'd gone over Eve Perry's offer.

"Do you think Lauren's that good?" Mr. Wing asked.

Coach Knudson's eyes met Lauren's. "Yes."

Putting her coffee cup down carefully, Lauren's mother said, "I think this is something the whole family needs to hear about—and discuss." She stood up and went to get Lisa, Lacey, and Bryan, who were in the backyard playing kickball with Lacey's soccer ball.

Mr. Wing looked at his oldest daughter. "Do *you* think you're good enough?"

"Yes," said Lauren firmly.

They sat silent again, until the rest of the family had gathered in the kitchen. Mrs. Wing scooped Lisa up to sit on her lap. Bryan leaned against the counter. Lacey settled in the chair next to Lauren, holding her soccer ball.

"What?" Lacey said.

At a nod from Mrs. Wing, Coach Knudson told the others about Lauren's offer from Eve Perry and the Silver Springs Skating Club. She'd barely finished before Bryan leaned forward to tug on Lauren's hair. "Good going," he said.

"That's great," said Lacey. "I mean, I think it is." She glanced at Coach Knudson, as if she was worried about hurting the coach's feelings.

"I'm the one who recommended that Eve take a look at Lauren," Coach Knudson said, guessing what Lacey was thinking. "I think your sister has what it takes to go all the way to the top, and I think Eve can help her get there—even more than I can."

"Is Lauren going to leave home?" Lisa asked, scowling fiercely at Coach Knudson.

"No. But Silver Springs is almost an hour away in good weather," Coach Knudson said. "A six o'clock lesson time means getting up at four-thirty in the morning. Every weekday morning, if I know Coach Perry. And that doesn't include practice time, and the additional training I think she'll want you to do, Lauren."

Lauren was stunned. She hadn't thought about that.

Coach Knudson turned to Mr. Wing. "And whoever drives Lauren to practice is going to have to learn how to use the Zamboni to resurface the ice, since it will be before the rink officially opens."

Lauren's father laughed unexpectedly. "I always wanted to drive one of those things," he said.

Then the room was silent again. Coach Knudson took a last sip from her coffee cup and rose to her feet. "I know it's a lot to think about, but you should consider this offer very, very seriously. It's the chance of a lifetime. With Regionals approaching, you don't want to waste any time."

Mr. Wing nodded. "I understand," he said. "We'll talk it over as a family and let you know."

He walked with Coach Knudson to the front door. But Lauren remained in her chair, staring down at her tightly clasped hands. She was too amazed to be happy.

Her mother said, "Bryan, time to set the table. Lisa, you're helping him tonight."

"And Lauren and I are doing the dishes. I know, I know." Lacey groaned.

"We can talk about this at dinner," Mrs. Wing went on. Lauren didn't move. She wasn't sure she *could* talk about it. She also wasn't sure she'd be able to eat any dinner while her whole life was being decided.

Mr. Wing took a brownie and passed the plate. "You haven't said very much, Lauren." Bryan went for two, then handed the plate to Lauren.

She picked the smallest one, put it down,

and forgot about it. "All those lessons," Lauren said. "They'll be expensive."

"Yes," agreed Mr. Wing. He paused. "We have some savings. And the restaurant is always busier during the summer tourist season."

"Will that be enough?" Lauren asked. This wasn't a fairy tale come true after all. In the fairy tales, there never was a problem.

"I don't know," her father said. He glanced across at Mrs. Wing. "I'll have to talk to the bookkeeper to see how workable it is."

"And the bookkeeper will see if she can work out a budget," said Mrs. Wing.

"You can have my allowance!" Lisa burst out.

Lauren bit her lip. "That's okay, Lisa."

"But you can," Lisa insisted.

Lauren poked at her own brownie. Anything chocolate for dessert normally wouldn't last two seconds on her plate. But tonight the brownie might as well have been her most unfavorite food, broccoli.

"Four-thirty in the morning," Lauren's mother said.

"That's disgusting," Bryan said. "Can I have your brownie, Lauren?"

"Sure," she said.

He snatched it up as if it were an escaping hockey puck and ate half of it in one bite.

"Chew your food, Bryan," Mrs. Wing said automatically.

"I vote yes," Bryan said. "But only if *I* don't have to get up at four-thirty in the morning."

"Me, too," Lacey said.

"Me, three," added Lisa.

Lauren picked up silverware and glasses. Now it was up to her parents.

But Mrs. Wing didn't vote, not yet. She said, "Bryan, can you get Lisa ready for bed? I'll be right up."

Bryan caught Lisa, tucked her under one arm, and carried her out of the room as she shrieked and kicked.

"I guess I'd better go help Lacey," Lauren said.

Her father said, "Your mother and I need to talk this over and think about it some more."

"I know," said Lauren. She paused, then

added, "But if I could work with Coach Perry, Dad—it would be like a dream come true. Like a, well, like a fairy tale. Or a miracle, even."

Her father smiled. "I know, Lauren. But dreams, fairy tales, even miracles, sometimes they don't just happen. They take work. They require sacrifices."

"I could get a job," Lauren burst out. She knew as she said it how impossible that was.

Her father and her mother exchanged glances. Her mother said, "You're too young, Lauren. And if you were skating all the time, when would you have time to work? In fact, with the schedule Coach Knudson has outlined, I'm worried you won't have time to do your homework."

"I will! I'll do my homework. I'll make even better grades. I'll do *anything*." Lauren hadn't meant to beg, but somehow she couldn't help herself.

Mrs. Wing said, "I know. But right now, all you need to do is go help Lacey with the dishes."

At least they haven't said no, thought Lauren. She began to rinse plates and hand them to Lacey to load into the dishwasher.

"I couldn't get up at four-thirty in the morning," Lacey greeted Lauren. "Not even for soccer."

"Not even if you had a chance to play on the Olympic team some day?" Lauren said.

Lacey stopped, holding a dish up, her eyes wide with surprise. "Who said anything about the Olympics?" she asked. "Did Coach Knudson? Or that Perry coach?"

"She said I should call her Eve," said Lauren, feeling herself blush a little. She'd never really talked about her dream of being an Olympic figure skater. "No, she didn't. But she's coached Olympic skaters before. Lots of them. She won't coach someone unless she thinks they could be really, really good."

"Oh," said Lacey. She looked at Lauren. "Wow. Hey, maybe we'll all get to go to the Olympics someday. I hope it's someplace good."

"Yeah," said Lauren. She didn't want to talk about that part of her dream. One thing at a time. First, she had to be able to work with Eve Perry.

12

"Lauren? Lauren?"

Lauren jumped. She stared at Ms. Campbell, her language arts teacher. "Will you read the next paragraph, please?" Ms. Campbell asked.

"Uh . . ." Lauren ran her finger down the page. They were reading *Julie of the Wolves*, a book Lauren loved. But she hadn't been paying attention. Her thoughts had not been on Julie in Alaska, but almost as far away.

Walking between the desks, Ms. Campbell stopped, peered over Lauren's shoulder, then pointed. "There," she said.

Someone snickered.

Lauren cleared her throat and began to read.

But when Ms. Campbell called on Lauren a second time and Lauren didn't know the answer, Ms. Campbell raised her eyebrows. "Are you with us today, Lauren?" she said.

"Sorry," Lauren mumbled as several more kids snickered and stared at her. She'd been unable to concentrate all day.

When the class was over, Lauren jumped up and raced out of the room. Normally, Ms. Campbell's class was one of her favorites, but today she was relieved when it ended.

One more class, she told herself, hurrying down the hall. One more class and then it's time for my lesson. If she could just get out on the ice, she could forget her worries. If she could just skate, everything would be better.

Lauren had never been more wrong.

Lauren stepped out of her spin and tottered dizzily across the ice.

"Again," said Coach Knudson. "You've got a good centered spin, Lauren. Use it."

Lauren did the spin again. Why couldn't she do a simple spin, one of the first spins she'd ever mastered? She did it again, and again, and finally Coach Knudson said, "Take a break. It looks like you're just practicing your mistakes. Get some water and we'll work on something else." The coach turned to Annie and Danielle.

Lauren skated to rinkside, snagged her water bottle, and took a drink. This is only the worst lesson of my life, she thought.

She was relieved that Eve Perry couldn't see her now. The coach would probably take back her offer, realize what a huge mistake she'd made.

No, Lauren told herself firmly. It wasn't a mistake.

A little voice said, *not like the mistake you made leaving the window open and letting Lutz out.* Lauren squeezed her eyes shut. Lutz. She missed him so much. She missed him sitting on her bed, watching her with bored amusement as she did her homework, stretching up to bat at her pencil from time to time. She missed him at night, curled on her bed. She missed him in the morning, missed waking up to his purr next to her ear.

But missing him wouldn't bring him back. Two weeks had passed, and there had been no sign of Lutz. A thunderstorm had torn away most of the "Lost Cat" signs.

They'd put an ad in the lost-and-found section of the *Pine Creek Free Press*, but that hadn't helped either.

Lutz. Lauren shook her head to shake the thoughts of him away. She went back out on the ice, resolving to work twice as hard. But no matter how hard she tried, she just kept going in wobbly circles like a broken top.

Finally Coach Knudson looked at her watch. "Okay, that's it for today. Lauren, could I see you for a minute?"

Lauren nodded. Shooting her curious looks, Danielle and Annie skated away to practice some more.

Coach Knudson said, "I talked to your father today."

They said no, Lauren thought, her heart plummeting to the soles of her skates.

"He asked me a lot of good questions. I wondered if you had any," her coach went on.

"N-noo," Lauren paused. "But I hadn't—I mean, I wanted to say thank you."

"Don't thank me yet," Coach Knudson said.

The coach turned to greet her next class and Lauren skated out onto the ice to practice.

"So what did she want?" Annie skidded to a hockey stop in front of Lauren, sending up a little spray of ice shavings.

"Pretty fancy," commented Danielle, slowing down in a more sedate manner. To Lauren she said, "Are you in trouble?"

"No. Not exactly. But I have something I have to tell you guys."

"What? *What*?" Annie asked.

"Not here," Lauren said, looking around at the bobbing, weaving, swooping skaters. "I'm tired of ice skating."

"Tired of skating?" Annie pretended to rub her ears. "Am I hearing right?"

"Okay. Then how about ice cream?" said Danielle.

Lauren hesitated for a moment. She had some allowance left for the week, but now more than ever, every cent counted. On the other hand, she needed to talk to her friends. And the ice cream would taste good.

"Let's go," she agreed.

The Scoop Rink, which was next door to the Pine Creek Skating Rink, was empty. Danielle got two scoops of Rocky Road, Annie picked butter pecan, and Lauren, after a moment's hesitation, decided on a single-scoop chocolate sundae with hot fudge and nuts.

They settled in at a table by the window and ate in silence for a moment. "This is sooo good," Danielle said. She grinned wickedly. "And I don't care if I spoil my appetite for dinner."

"That could never happen to me," declared Annie.

"Me, either," Lauren said, a little thickly. She licked the fudge from her spoon. Suddenly, her appetite was returning.

"So, now that I'm not *deeply* ice-cream deprived," Danielle said, "what's the scoop?"

Annie groaned at Danielle's humor. "Feeble," she said.

Danielle rolled her eyes. "Tell," she ordered Lauren. "Or else."

"Okay. This is the deal." Lauren took a deep breath. "Eve Perry has invited me to join the Silver Springs Skating Club."

Annie's mouth dropped open.

Danielle fell back in her chair and threw her arm across her forehead.

At last Annie said, "Eve *Perry*? You? When? What did she say? What . . ."

"Start at the beginning. Don't leave a single thing out," Danielle interrupted.

Lauren told them about her meeting with Coach Perry after the Pine Creek competition, about Coach Knudson's visit to her house, and about her conversation with her parents after Coach Knudson left.

"Unbelievable!" cried Annie. "Triple-toe-loop fantastic."

"So when do you start?" Danielle asked.

"Maybe never," Lauren said softly.

"What?" Danielle fell back again, in shock, and this time she wasn't just acting. "You're kidding. This is not funny."

"I'm serious. It's a huge change. And it costs lots of money," Lauren said.

"Your parents will agree. They'll have to agree." Annie said.

Danielle took another bite of rocky road, then pushed the dish of ice cream away. "The Silver Springs Club," she said softly. "Eve Perry."

"It'll work out, Lauren," Annie said. "I know it will."

"Yeah," said Danielle. She didn't look at Lauren now. She was studying her spoon.

Annie wrinkled her nose, making the faint scattering of freckles run together. "But if you take lessons with Coach Perry, you won't be taking lessons with us anymore, will you?"

"No," Danielle said. "Weren't you listening, Annie? She'll be going to Silver Springs every morning, for her private lessons with Coach Perry."

"I'll still practice with you guys in the afternoons," Lauren said. "We'll still have competitions together."

"Better wait and see what your new coach says before making any promises." Danielle looked at the clock above the ice cream counter.

"Mom'll be here any minute to pick me up. I've gotta go."

"Yeah," said Annie. She took a huge bite of her butter pecan.

But to Lauren's and Annie's surprise, Danielle didn't wait. She stood up. "See you," she said. With that, she slung her skate bag over her shoulder and walked out of the Scoop Rink.

Annie's brows knitted together. "Whoa," she said. "What's Danielle's problem?"

"I don't know," said Lauren. But she had an idea—an idea that made her unhappy, made everything that had happened in the last few days that much more unsettling, if it was true.

Annie, finishing the last of her butter pecan ice cream, spoke Lauren's uneasy feelings aloud. "I think I know," she said and shook her head. "Looks like Danielle is really jealous."

"I never thought Danielle could be jealous of me," Lauren said. And for the first time Lauren didn't feel like finishing her ice cream.

13

Math is easy, thought Lauren. Life is hard. Chin propped on one hand, she sat staring at her homework. But even math, usually one of her better subjects, wasn't adding up today.

Lauren shifted slightly in her chair and made a face. Life is hard, math is hard, plus I'm sore, she thought. Ugh. All those less-than-perfect spins at practice had worked muscles that weren't used to being jerked around. In addition, her crash landings on the unforgiving ice had tattooed her with bruises.

"Pillows," Lauren said aloud. "I need pillows." She bagged the two pillows from her bed, sat on one and put the other behind her back. She leaned over her homework, wincing a little. "If a plane leaves from Chicago," she read, "traveling five-hundred miles per hour . . ."

And goes to the World Championships in Europe, her mind added. With me on it. And other world-famous skaters. And Eve.

No. Math. She had to think about math. Her glance strayed to the spot on the bed where Lutz had always sat. She looked quickly away.

She heard the phone ring. A minute later, Lacey poked her head through the bedroom door. "It's for you," she said. Relief flooded Lauren. Maybe it was Danielle. Maybe she could talk to Danielle and if she did, maybe life would be a little less confusing. Maybe even math wouldn't be so hard.

But Annie's voice crackled over the receiver. "Yes or no?" she demanded.

"Neither," Lauren said. "They haven't decided yet." Lauren didn't have to ask what the question was. She knew that Annie was talking about her parents' decision about Eve Perry.

"Mom wants to talk to Eve, so she and Dad are going down to Saratoga tomorrow."

Annie groaned loudly. "Death by toe pick. How can you stand it?"

"I don't have a choice," said Lauren.

"Are you going?" Anne asked.

"No. No, I'm going to practice. After today's lesson, I need it," Lauren said.

"Maybe that's better," said Annie. "See, it proves you're way, *way* serious about skating.

"Thanks, Annie," Lauren said, laughing in spite of herself.

"Any time," Annie said. "See you at the rink."

At lunch, Rebecca leaned over and waved her hand in Lauren's face. "It's a nice lunchroom window," she said, "but I don't see anything so amazing about the tree."

Lauren turned dazed eyes on Rebecca.

Rebecca held out her hand. "Hi. I'm Beck. Are you in there?"

"Sorry," said Lauren sheepishly.

"So what's going on?"

"Nothing," said Lauren.

"Yeah. Would that be skating nothing, or some other kind of nothing?" Rebecca asked.

Lauren sighed. "Skating," she said.

"Not that I had to be a genius to guess," Rebecca said. "Tell me."

"Well, I had the worst lesson of my entire life yesterday. I wouldn't be surprised if Coach Knudson just fired me."

"Coaches don't fire students, they just quit coaching them," said Rebecca.

"It's just . . . you remember Eve Perry?" Lauren asked.

"That famous coach type? Sure," Rebecca said.

"Well, she's asked me if I want to be her student," Lauren said.

"Cool," said Rebecca. "Tell me everything."

So Lauren did. When she had finished, Rebecca said, "This could change your whole life."

"I know," Lauren said, and for a moment saw herself at center ice at the World Championships.

Rebecca was obviously having a far different vision. "How are you going to stay awake in school if you go to the rink at six A.M. every morning?"

"I'll go to bed early," Lauren said. "And I'm

going to have to rearrange my schedule."

"If you do, we won't have homeroom toge-ther, probably," Rebecca said.

"Oh," said Lauren. "You're right." She hadn't considered that part of it.

Rebecca looked at Lauren, her expression troubled. Then she said, "Well, good luck, Lauren. I think. If it's what you really want, I hope you get it."

Lauren looked back at Rebecca, her own expression somber. "It is what I want, Beck. More than anything in the world."

Rebecca gave a tiny nod. Then she said, "You know, it'd be a cool science project. Figure Skating and the Law of Gravity."

Lauren nodded. She understood that Rebecca didn't want to talk about it anymore. And somehow, Lauren didn't either.

Danielle slammed her locker shut just as Lauren came in.

"Danielle. Hi!" Lauren said.

"Hi," said Danielle. She spun the lock on the locker.

"I hope I do better today than I did yesterday," said Lauren. "That was the worst. The absolute worst. A total ouch-athon."

"It happens," said Danielle. Her voice was flat.

"And I was totally sore last night," said Lauren. "Ice is supposed to help when you're sore, but what do you do when it was ice that made you sore in the first place?"

Zipping her warm-up jacket, Danielle smiled a little at Lauren's attempt at humor.

"Let me get my skates and I'll walk out with you," Lauren said.

But Danielle picked up her water bottle and said, "Don't hurry. I'll see you on the ice."

Lauren stared after her. This is another part they leave out of the fairy tales, she thought. With a sigh, Lauren picked up her own skates and headed out of the locker room.

How can I make Danielle stop being jealous? she wondered. She thought of the times she'd been envious of one of Danielle's wonderful new skating outfits or of Annie's ability to make supersonic jumps or even of Erica, who could have private lessons and private ice time.

But never had it occurred to Lauren that someone might be jealous of her.

At rinkside, she put on her skates and skated out onto the ice. Her parents were meeting with Coach Perry right now, she thought. What if they said no?

"Lauren." Coach Knudson's voice was loud.

Lauren looked up.

"It's a nice pose," Coach Knudson said, with a little smile. "But from there I'd like to see you skate into a double toe loop."

"Oh!" said Lauren, her cheeks burning. "Right."

As she executed the toe loop, her muscles protested. She imagined them saying, "Hey, give us a break! You just banged us against the ice for hours last night!"

She landed upright—barely. She grimaced, and her sore muscles knotted.

To Lauren's relief, Coach Knudson didn't point out the errors in the jump. She just nodded.

"Now, Danielle," Coach Knudson said. She waited. "Danielle?"

Danielle blinked, startled, then pushed off as if someone were chasing her. She rushed into her moves, and when the sequence was done, Coach Knudson said, "Danielle, if I didn't know better, I'd think you were clowning around."

"I'm a little out of rhythm today," said Danielle.

"Slow down," Coach Knudson answered. "You're not going to get back in sync by over-skating. Annie, let's see what you're up to this afternoon."

In contrast to Lauren and Danielle, Annie skated like an ice princess.

Coach Knudson smiled. "That's what I like to see," she said. Then she put Danielle and Lauren to work on basics, something she did when she felt as if students were not focused enough. Annie went to work on her toe loop.

After the lesson, as they headed for the locker room, Annie said, "I just want to thank you guys for making me look so good today. I mean, neither of you was on the planet, you know?"

"I know," said Lauren.

Danielle said, "Lauren has more important things to think about than one of our old lessons. Don't you, Lauren?"

Lauren opened her mouth to deny it. Then she stopped. "Right now, it's the most important thing in the world. My parents are meeting with Eve Perry right this minute."

"You'd be distracted, too," Annie told Danielle. "You know you would."

"Maybe," said Danielle. She slammed her locker door. "But I guess I'll never find out." With that, she was gone.

"Jealous," said Annie in her blunt way, as Danielle's footsteps faded away. "I am, too, I guess."

"Oh, Annie," said Lauren.

"It's dumb, I know," said Annie. "But listen, it's not like I hate you or anything. It's just that I wish it was me."

They were quiet for a minute as they finished changing out of their skating clothes. Then Annie gave Lauren a sideways glance and a grin.

"What?" said Lauren.

To Lauren's amazement, Annie stuck out her tongue and made a hideous face.

"Annie!" said Lauren.

"There. I feel better," said Annie. "I'll just do that whenever I need to, and it'll be fine. Now, listen up. You are in big, big trouble if you don't call me the moment your parents tell you yes."

14

"Hey! Where's the fire?" Bryan dodged into the grass as Lauren rode up the driveway on her bike. Lauren screeched to a stop.

She dropped the bike and put her hands on her knees, taking deep gulps of air. She'd chosen the hard way home, up the steepest, longest hills. That kept her from thinking about Danielle's jealous anger and Rebecca's lukewarm response to her big news.

And about Lutz. No. She wouldn't think about Lutz, probably lost forever, all because of her.

Bryan dribbled back onto the driveway and

put a shot up in the hoop above the garage door. "Wanna shoot some?" he asked.

Lauren straightened up and looked around, fumbling with the strap of her bike helmet.

"They're not back yet," Bryan said. "They've got to pick Lisa up from her friend's house, and Lacey is still at soccer practice."

Lauren walked her bike into the garage. What was taking them so long? Was it good or was it bad that they hadn't come home yet from their meeting with Eve Perry?

Bryan passed the basketball to Lauren as she came back out of the garage. He said, "You win, I set the table and do dishes tonight, I win, and you're the chore master."

"You're on." Lauren never could resist a challenge. She jammed toward the basket.

An hour later, in the near darkness, Lauren and Bryan finished a killer game.

"I'll just watch television while you set the table," Bryan said grandly.

"You got lucky," Lauren said.

"Yeah, yeah, yeah," said Bryan.

They went into the house and Lauren began

to put dishes and silverware on the table. She had just put the last fork in place when the back door opened.

"We're home!" cried Lisa, skipping. Lacey followed Lisa into the kitchen.

Lauren froze, all her attention on her mother's face.

Mrs. Wing wasn't smiling. She looked tired. Her eyes met Lauren's. "Your father's bringing in pizza," she said. "Lisa, go wash your hands and call Bryan. We need to have a family meeting."

I don't believe this, thought Lauren, as she watched her family around the dinner table.

Bryan, Lacey, and Lisa were grabbing for the pizza as if it were just another family dinner.

Lauren's mother took a slice and put it on her plate. Lauren's father did the same, and mechanically, Lauren followed suit.

But she never took her gaze from her parents.

Mr. Wing cleared his throat. He looked at Mrs. Wing. She nodded slightly.

"Eve Perry is very impressive," Lauren's father said.

"And a very persuasive woman," her mother

added. "She could be a lawyer."

"Did she talk about what a great skater Lauren is?" Bryan said. It sounded as if he'd said, "Id she alk about at a ate ater auren is," because he'd just taken an enormous bite of pizza.

Automatically Mrs. Wing said, "Bryan, don't talk with your mouth full. And yes, we spent a lot of time talking about Lauren's skating. In addition to a number of other things." She paused. She glanced at Lauren's father. He nodded slightly.

"So this is the deal," Lauren's mother said. She took a deep breath.

And at that moment, the front doorbell rang.

Lauren wanted to scream.

Mrs. Wing stood up. "Who could that be?" she wondered aloud.

Lauren's mother went down the hall to the front door. They heard her open it.

Then they heard her say, "Oh, thank goodness. You've found him!"

Bryan leaped up so fast his chair tipped over.

"It's Lutz!" Lacey shouted, shooting up from

her seat and running toward the door.

A mad stampede followed, including even Lauren's normally calm father.

Lauren was the last to reach the hall. Lutz, as fat and shiny as ever, was clutched in Lisa's arms, purring.

"Lutz!" said Lauren, tears filling her eyes and spilling down her cheeks. "Oh, Lutz."

Lutz turned up the volume of his purr and dug his claws into Lauren's shoulder. But she didn't care. She buried her face in his fur.

She looked up to see a man, woman, and young boy standing in the doorway. "We're so grateful you found him," Mrs. Wing was saying. "Won't you come in? And there's the reward . . ."

But the man was shaking his head. "We can't stay. And we don't want the reward. Stephen has something he'd like to say to you."

The boy stepped forward. He looked over at Lutz. His forehead wrinkled and then he said softly, "I'm sorry."

"Sorry? For finding our cat?" Bryan said.

"No." Stephen's mother put her hand on her son's shoulder. "We're the reason your cat's been missing so long. He's been living in our toolshed. We hadn't been out to it for a couple of weeks, but when I went out there this afternoon to check on something, I found your cat."

"I found him!" Stephen cried out. "I thought he was lost, so I put him in the shed and fed him. I named him Silver King."

"Stephen's been wanting a cat for a long time. But we didn't think he was ready for the responsibility," Stephen's father explained.

"I *am*," Stephen insisted.

That seemed to be true. Lutz appeared none the worse for his two weeks in the toolshed.

Lauren smiled at Stephen, as the ache that had been lodged in her heart for so long dissolved. "I can tell you took good care of him," she said.

"See?" Stephen said.

"But it was wrong of you to keep him at all," his father said.

Stephen hung his head. "I know," he said.

"He's back. That's what counts," Lacey said. She'd been petting Lutz nonstop, as had Lisa.

Shifting Lutz into Lacey's arms, Lauren took a step forward. "When you're ready for a cat of your own," she said, "I know just the person you should talk to. Her name is Rebecca, and she and her family rescue cats that need homes."

Stephen's sad face brightened a little. He glanced at his parents hopefully, then back at Lauren. "Really?" he said.

"Really," said Lauren. "I'll write the number down for you." She handed the piece of paper to Stephen's parents.

"Thank you again," said Mrs. Wing.

"Good-bye, Silver King," Stephen said. He followed his parents down the walk to the car, looking back over his shoulder.

Mrs. Wing closed the door and ran her hand through her hair. "Well, Lutz, welcome home," she said. "You are just in time to hear a Wing family decision."

15

Lutz was purring on Lauren's lap. Lisa kept leaning over to offer him treats. Lacey petted him after practically every bite of pizza, and even Bryan reached over from time to time to scratch the big gray cat's ears.

The decision Lauren's parents had made about Eve was still very, very important to Lauren. But somehow, holding Lutz, she didn't feel as if her life would be totally over if they said no. Having Eve Perry offer her the chance was part of the fairy tale. Having Lutz come home was another part of it.

Her father cleared his throat.

"First, Lauren, Coach Perry went to a lot of

effort to make us understand just how much harder you'll have to work. She stressed repeatedly that all the talent in the world is useless unless you're willing to be completely devoted to training. I know Coach Knudson has told you this many times before, but I wanted to say it again. According to Coach Perry, she demands total commitment."

Mr. Wing paused and glanced around the table. "She said the commitment had to come not just from the skater, but from the whole family. Does everyone understand that?"

"Got it," Lacey said. "Team Lauren, right?"

Mr. Wing nodded, then looked at his oldest daughter. "That means you, Lauren, will be up almost every morning before dawn—and so will I. You'll have to go to bed early, almost with Lisa."

"I can help with that!" Lisa said.

"We will have to economize even more. Pizza, yes, steak dinners, no." Her father smiled and so did everyone else. Pizza was the dinner of choice over steak for the Wings any day.

"In addition, you'll have to start working out with weights. . . ."

"Count me in on that," Bryan said.

"And we'll all have to plan many of our weekends according to Lauren's training and competition schedule. And that's only the beginning."

Mr. Wing stopped. "Well?" he said.

Lauren looked at her family. She said softly, "I can do this. I know I can. I want it more than I want anything in the world." She looked down at Lutz. He gave her a golden, mysterious cat look. "Well, almost anything," she amended.

Her father said, "All right. Bryan?"

"Why not?" said Bryan.

"I vote yes," agreed Lacey.

"Me, too," said Lisa, raising her hand as if she were in her kindergarten class.

Then Lauren's mother sighed. "And your grades have to stay up, Lauren. That's the number one priority."

"I know," said Lauren.

"Okay," Mrs. Wing said. "Okay."

"That's it, then," said Mr. Wing.

Lauren felt the world tilt a little inside her. But her father went on as if her whole life had not just changed. "We'll talk to your school tomorrow. In order for you to take the early-morning lessons, your schedule will have to be rearranged." He paused, then added, "You start with Coach Perry this Monday at six A.M."

Lauren couldn't hold back anymore. She leaped from her seat. "Thank you!" she said. "Oh, thank you."

"Mrrrow!" protested Lutz, as he landed on the floor with a solid thump.

"Sorry, Lutz," Lauren said.

Unwilling to forgive her so easily, he stalked out of the room, his tail in the air.

They watched him go in silence. Then they all began to laugh. Lauren, feeling giddy and relieved at the same time, laughed loudest of all. Lutz was home, and she was happier even than a princess in a fairy tale. She fell back onto her chair.

Suddenly, Lauren leaped to her feet again. "Omigosh," she said. "I've got to call Rebecca and tell her Lutz is home! And Annie and . . ." She ran out of the room without finishing the sentence. She'd tell them the good news.

But she wasn't sure yet what she would do about Danielle.

Rebecca took the news of Lutz's return with amazing calm. "I knew he'd be back!" she exclaimed. "I even made him a new collar to wear."

Lauren told Rebecca the whole story. She also told her about her parents' decision to allow her to skate for Eve Perry. Rebecca's congratulations were sincere. A wave of happiness washed over Lauren. Everything was changing, but at least one thing wasn't: Rebecca was still her true-blue best friend.

Annie's reaction was very different. Even holding the phone at arm's length, Lauren could still hear Annie's shrieks.

Lauren grinned as Annie said, "Lauren, this is most totally excellent, amazing, and wonderful. Lutz back and skating for Eve Perry! Are you excited?"

"What do you think?" Lauren said. "But I still don't believe it's true."

"Are you going to call Danielle?" Annie asked.

Lauren hesitated. She should call Danielle, but she dreaded talking to her.

"Maybe it'll be better if I tell Danielle when I see her," Lauren said. "Tomorrow at our lesson."

As Lauren hung up the phone, she felt a sinking feeling in her stomach. What was she going to say to Danielle?

16

"That's it," Coach Knudson said. She held up her hands and applauded. "An excellent lesson, all three of you."

"And our last with Lauren." Annie sighed.

Danielle didn't say anything.

Coach Knudson smiled. "We'll still see each other at competitions and at practice. Lauren, good luck." Instead of hugging Lauren, as Lauren half expected, Coach Knudson held out her hand.

Feeling suddenly much older, Lauren took the coach's hand. "Thank you," she said.

"Yeah, good luck," Danielle echoed. She took a step toward Lauren and for a moment

Lauren thought that Danielle would hug her. But then Danielle stepped back and extended her hand, too. Instead of making Lauren feel grown up, this made her feel awkward.

She looked at Danielle steadily, then held out her own hand. "Thank you, Danielle," she said. "Good luck to you, too," as if she and Danielle were practically strangers.

Danielle blushed, dropped Lauren's hand, and said, "Well, I've got to practice." She pushed off and glided away across the ice, seeming to concentrate entirely on her crossovers.

Coach Knudson picked up her skate bag, put her clipboard into one of the side pockets, and walked briskly out of the rink.

"Want to practice spins some more?" Annie asked.

"No," Lauren said slowly. She was looking around the rink. Would it look different after her lessons with Eve? The rink was familiar and safe, her favorite place on earth for so many years. And now, that would never be the same.

"I think," Lauren went on slowly, "that I'm going to go home now."

Annie seemed to understand. "Okay," she said. She added, "Don't worry about Danielle. She'll get over it."

Would she? Lauren wondered. She didn't know what to believe. "Maybe," she said aloud. She forced herself to smile, although inside, she felt suddenly goopy, to use one of Lisa's words. She leaned over and hugged Annie fiercely. "I'll miss you. I'll miss you both," she whispered.

Annie hugged Lauren back so hard that Lauren said, "Oof." They stepped apart and regarded one another. Then with her gremlin smile Annie said, "Ten triple toe loops! You'll be around. It's not like you're moving to another planet."

"Right." But the goopy feeling inside wasn't going away.

As Lauren left the building, she passed Erica on the steps outside. Lauren nodded. Even more than usual, she didn't feel like talking to Erica.

But Erica blocked her way. "I hear you are going to leave Coach Knudson," she said.

Lauren shrugged. "Something like that."

"I guess Eve Perry felt sorry for you," Erica persisted.

"You can believe what you want," said Lauren.

"I can believe what's true," Erica shot back.

"Whatever," said Lauren. She tried to push past Erica, but Erica put out her hand.

"You're not that good, Lauren. It won't take Eve Perry long to find out. You in your stupid homemade outfits and ratty old skates . . . puh-lease! She'll know she's made a big mistake and then she'll . . ."

Lauren's cheeks burned at Erica's words. But before she could speak, footsteps clattered down the steps. Danielle stopped beside Lauren and faced Erica. "Your fancy outfits and expensive skates didn't make Eve Perry want to coach you, did they?" Danielle interrupted Erica's tirade.

"Who asked you?" Erica snapped.

Ignoring her question, Danielle rushed on. "You know, if you weren't such a rotten person, maybe you'd be a better skater."

"Like you'd know what a good skater is," Erica said.

"Well, I know what a rotten person is. And only a rotten, jealous person would say what you've just said."

"Jealous!" Erica's voice was shrill. "I don't *think* so." She shoved past Danielle so hard that Danielle lost her balance and had to grab Lauren to keep from falling.

Lauren suddenly found her voice. "Hey, Erica," she called. "I just thought you'd like to know . . ."

Erica spun, seeming to brace herself.

"I found my cat," Lauren heard herself say.

That rendered Erica speechless. Her mouth opened, then closed. Then the door of the rink slammed shut behind her.

"'I found my cat'? Wow, that's a knockout punch," Danielle said. Then the words registered. "You found Lutz? That's *great*, Lauren! I'm so glad."

"Yeah. Me, too," Lauren said. "Some people had adopted him sort of by accident. They brought him home last night."

"Good old Lutz. Cats always land on their feet, you know." Danielle paused, and then said,

"I guess that Erica's not ever going to be a cat, on or off the ice, huh?"

It took a moment for Lauren to get it. When she did, she couldn't help laughing. "Thanks, Danielle," she said. "For standing up for me."

"Yeah, well, I was coming out and I heard her and what could I do?" Danielle shrugged.

"I'm going to miss you," Lauren said.

Danielle looked down at her feet and said to her toes, "What I said about Erica. It's true. About me, I mean. I've been jealous of you. I wish it was me. I wish it could be all of us, but most of all I wish it was me. I'm sorry."

"Why are you sorry? I'd wish it was me if I was you," Lauren said.

"Would you?" Danielle still seemed to be talking to her toes.

"You bet. I'm glad when you win, but I'm even happier when I do. And you're the same way. And so is Annie."

"I guess you're right." Danielle raised her head. "I've been a total, miserable, first-class, award-winning creep, haven't I?"

Again, Lauren couldn't help but laugh. That

sounded more like the old Danielle. "Well, not that bad," Lauren said. She smiled wickedly. "Don't forget Erica."

"Oh, *thanks*," Danielle said. She pretended to stagger back, clutching her heart. "That hurts."

A car horn sounded. It was Danielle's father, picking her up after her lesson.

"See you later," said Danielle. She paused. "Won't I?"

"You better believe it," Lauren answered.

Danielle grabbed Lauren by both shoulders and made kissy sounds next to each cheek. "That's what you do when you're famous," she explained.

"I'll remember that," Lauren said. "It might come in handy."

Grinning, Danielle waved and clattered down the steps to the waiting car.

Lauren waved until Danielle was out of sight.

17

"Mrrow!" Lutz tumbled from the bed as Lauren sprang toward the alarm clock. She punched it off and waited a moment.

She heard Lacey shift in her bed. But Lisa slept on, making little whistling noises.

In the dark, Lauren shuffled to the door of the room, opened it, and slipped out into the hall. Only the night-light was burning. Lutz trailed her as Lauren went into the bathroom, intrigued by this unusual human activity. He sat on the toilet seat and watched as she washed her face.

"My first lesson with Eve Perry today, Lutz," she whispered.

He regarded her steadily, then stretched out

his hind foot and began to wash it.

Lauren laughed softly. "I wish I was that flexible," she said. "I could do great tricks."

She heard the soft pad of footsteps, and then a rap on the door. "You up?" her father's voice inquired.

"It's me. I'm up," Lauren answered.

His footsteps receded. Lauren had taken her clothes into the bathroom the night before. She dressed quickly, still yawning, and hurried down the hall to the top of the stairs.

How quiet the house was and how dark! It felt so strange to be moving through the shadows. As she had done for almost longer than she could remember, she hopped to the bottom of the steps.

But this time, no Lisa waited at the bottom for her to award her a perfect score. Lisa was still deep in dreams and would be for almost three more hours.

Lauren paused, then went into the kitchen. Her father was pouring out a cup of tea into a travel mug. He filled a second mug for her.

"You have everything?" he asked.

"My bag is all packed," she answered. She had packed her skate bag and then repacked it the night before. Her schoolwork and new schedule were all in her backpack next to the skate bag.

He nodded. "Why don't you load your gear into the van. I'll be right behind you," he said.

She lugged the skate bag and pack out to the van parked in the driveway, and slung them into the back. A faint gray light was in the eastern sky, but everything else was dark, a sea of darkness with only streetlights like the masts of ships, and the light from the kitchen like a lighthouse on shore.

Shivering a little in the predawn chill, Lauren zipped her jacket up to her chin and slid into the van. She buckled her seat belt as her father came out. The kitchen light went out, and then his door opened. He slid in and handed her one mug and put a paper sack between the seats.

The van coughed and complained and then roared to life. It sounded so loud, Lauren half expected lights to come on in the houses around them.

But the only lights that came on were the headlights, and the world stayed still and dark as they backed out of the driveway.

"Look," said Lauren suddenly. "The newspaper." A truck was parked in front of a store, and a burly man in the back the truck was tossing bundles of newspapers onto the sidewalk.

"The paper carriers will be starting their routes soon," her father said.

Lauren yawned and took a sip of tea.

"Sleep a little," her father urged.

"I can't," she said. "I'm too excited."

He smiled but said nothing. Settling the travel mug into the holder, Lauren leaned her head against the seat and watched the streetlights flash by.

They turned onto the Northway. Lauren's head tipped back and before she knew it, she had fallen asleep.

She awoke with a start as her father slowed down. The sky was more gray than black. Her father reached over and picked up the paper bag and put it in her lap. "Your mother packed one for you," he said.

Lauren opened the bag. Inside she found a thermos of oatmeal, hot, with a packet of raisins and a packet of brown sugar. She also found a blueberry muffin spread with cream cheese, and a bottle of orange juice.

"Wow," Lauren said, "This is great." She pulled out a smaller sack and held it up. "David," she read, and then realized that it was her father's name.

"I think that's my breakfast," her father said. "And there's a thermos of hot tea by my seat. Could you refill my cup?"

"Absolutely," Lauren said.

Her father slowed down and turned off the Northway. The town they drove into was much bigger than Pine Creek. Lights were on now in many of the houses.

Her family would be waking up soon, she thought. Would Lisa miss her? Would Lacey wake up in time without Lauren there? Of course she would. Her mother would never let them oversleep.

She finished the last of her muffin. She wiped the utensils with a napkin and put them and the thermos into the paper bag.

The van slowed even more, and then turned.

Lauren looked up. Ahead, she saw the sign: Silver Springs Ice Rink. And then she saw the rink.

It gleamed in the morning sun.

Her father parked the van right out front as Lauren stared at the big new rink. "Time for our lessons," he said.

"Our?"

"You skate, I Zamboni," he said.

"Oh, right," she said.

With her father carrying her skate bag, they walked into the building together. It smelled new.

"I turn here," her father said, "I hope we'll have the ice cleared before your lesson starts. Your mother will pick you up after it is over."

"Okay," she said. Everything was happening so fast. For a moment, she wanted to cling to her father's hand as if she were Lisa.

But she wasn't five years old. She raised her chin as if she were at center ice. "Thanks," she said.

He put his arm around her shoulder and hugged her briefly. "Good luck, Lauren Wing," he said. He put down her skate bag, pushed open the door, and disappeared down a hallway.

Another door opened ahead of her.

A small, imperious figure in a yellow jacket stepped out. She raised her hand in a sharp motion. "Ah," Eve Perry said. "Lauren. Good. You are on time. Being on time is a good beginning." Still speaking, the coach wheeled and trotted down the hall. "They say 'Punctuality is the courtesy of kings,' you know. There's the locker room. Come along, come along, the ice is waiting."

"Coming," said Lauren. She smiled, picked up her skate bag, and walked toward the ice.

Ask Michelle!

If you have a question that you would like to ask Michelle, visit http://www.skatingdreams.com

What inspired you to become a figure skater?

When I was five years old, my sister, Karen, and I always went to watch my brother, Ron, play hockey. I was the youngest, and my parents said I was too little to skate. I begged and begged till finally my parents gave in.

I loved being on the ice. But it was a couple years later, when I was seven, that something magical happened to me. My real moment of inspiration—the one that changed my life forever—came while I was watching the 1988 Winter Olympics on TV. When I saw Brian Boitano skating for the gold medal, I saw the life I wanted to have. I've never doubted my decision to go all the way with my sport, and every time I step onto the ice I get inspired all over again.

How do you deal with the pressure of having to practice and perform all the time?

There can be pressure in a life like mine. I have lots of help dealing with it, though. My family is extremely supportive of me. They do more than cheer for me when I'm on the ice. They're always reminding me that, as important as skating is to me, it's only one part of my life. They're always encouraging me to do lots of other things: to study hard, read a lot, spend time with my friends, and keep my eyes open to the world around me. They've always said: "Work hard, be yourself, and have fun."

How does it feel to be figure skating in front of all those people?

At a big competition, the arena is full of people, TV cameras, noise, and intense excitement. That can be nerve-wracking and scary, if you let it. So before I step onto the ice, it's important that I concentrate and try to focus on one thing only: skating.

If I concentrate really hard, by the time my music starts I feel like I'm in a different world. I'm excited but calm. I can take everything in without getting nervous. The music gets inside of me. All the noises in the arena invigorate me. Then the crowd doesn't seem scary anymore. I can tell that they're on my side. They hold their breath before I do a big jump, and they relax and applaud when I land! Thousands of people seem to be feeling what I'm feeling. They give me courage. With all that energy lifting me up, I feel more like I'm flying than skating.

How do you pick out the costumes and music for your competitions?

When I am planning a routine for a competition, the music comes first. I look for music that hits a chord inside of me—in my heart. My coach, my choreographer, and I listen to lots and lots of CDs to find the piece of music that expresses a certain feeling. I don't always know what I want—but when I hear it, I know it!

Once we pick the music and choreograph the program, then we choose a costume that not only suits me best, but somehow expresses the same feelings we hear in the music. If it is dramatic music, then the costume will be dramatic. If the music is light and airy, then the costume will be flowing and seemingly weightless.

Skating is considered an "individual" sport, but really it's a team effort.

So, you want to be like Michelle?

That's easy!
Just pick up the new book series

MICHELLE KWAN
PRESENTS *Skating Dreams*

EACH BOOK CONTAINS:
- *Ask Michelle!*
Real questions from fans answered by Michelle.

- **Collectible Postcard**
A full-color photo of Michelle packed with fun facts about Michelle's stellar career!

Look for these future titles from the
Michelle Kwan Presents Skating Dreams series

SKATING DREAMS #3:   **SKATING DREAMS #4:**
Skating Backwards   *Champion's Luck*

AVAILABLE IN SEPTEMBER AND NOVEMBER 2000

Hyperion Books For Children   © Disne